Love Texas Style

Marty Tidwell
Nancy Connally
Christine Crocker
Jen FitzGerald
Nikki Hollaway
Mary Malcolm
L. A. Mitchell
Angi Morgan
Gina Lee Nelson
Beth Shriver
Arline Todd

Contact Information: info@thewildrosepress.com

Cover Art by *Rae Monet*

The Wild Rose Press

PO Box 708

Adams Basin, NY 14410-0706

Visit us at www.thewildrosepress.com

First Yellow Rose Edition, 2008

Print ISBN 1-60154-199-6

Published in the United States of America

Prickly Heat

by

Marty Tidwell

Dedication

This one's for Bill who always provides
the heat and leaves the prickly to me.
Any hero I write pales in comparison.

He left a yellow rose on the kitchen table, as if that would make everything okay. I stuck it in a vase and moved it onto the windowsill over the sink so I wouldn't have to see it constantly, but of course my eyes drifted to the damn flower every other minute.

Pete called himself a broken-down rodeo cowboy, but despite his slight limp, I had a hard time thinking of him as a broken-down anything. He was the strongest man I knew, not just physically, but emotionally, too. He'd held me up more than once over the years, and now when he was the one that needed something, I'd let him down. The rose was his way of saying he understood. Damn him.

I wasn't about to let myself off the hook that easily. I walked from the kitchen onto the screened-in back porch. The afternoon heat hit me in the face like the flat side of a cast iron skillet. The day was bright and sun-baked. The sky was cloudless and blue. The yard was parched and brown. And Pete's pick-up truck was still parked out by the barn. Before I lost my courage, I pushed open the back door and headed out to find him.

I dragged my feet, kicking up dust with every step, coating my cowboy boots with a layer of dried-out Texas soil. It hadn't rained in weeks and even the weeds looked thirsty.

"Pete?" As I approached the barn door, I called out a warning that I was about to invade his territory. The building might have been my property, but it belonged to him, body and soul. Pete was my foreman, but that didn't begin to explain what he was to me.

The Double M was the only home he'd ever known. His father, a tough old bird, had been the foreman before him, back when my dad ran a big herd. Both men, bless 'em, had passed on, leaving me to run things, and I missed them both every day. The ranch was about half its former size, parts of it sold off over the years to pay taxes, but Pete stayed on, still living in the small frame house up the hill from the main house.

1

These days we took in retired rodeo horses and ran camps for disadvantaged city kids. He considered himself just the hired help. But he was wrong. He was the heart of the operation. Lately, for him though, that didn't seem to be enough. I stepped inside and called again, "You in here, Pete?"

"I'm in back, Goldie. I'll be right there." His familiar voice echoed from deep inside the building, stirring up a tub of emotions in my gut that I didn't want to sort out. I'd been avoiding the truth about a lot of things lately, and now was as good a time as any to stop. I'd never thought about losing Pete, but if I kept pushing at him I would. He was a fact of life, like gravity or the wind. And if he went away I feared I might just float, unfettered, above the ground and blow about like cottonwood fluff on a summer day.

Maybe I was being mush-headed and lyrical, but if he ever left, I'd surely curl up and die. But this wasn't about me.

He stepped out of the back room and started my way. He was tall and broad and had a rolling gait that made me think inappropriate thoughts about long nights and four poster beds. That loose, languid walk was the result of an injury he'd suffered when a bull had taken exception to having him on his back a long time ago. His hip never healed right, but it didn't slow him down, either.

Shafts of light spilled in from the high windows and dust motes and bits of hay danced in the air, shimmering around him as he got closer. His white t-shirt was smeared with grease, and he wiped his hands on a rag and stuffed it in his back jeans pocket. He took his cowboy hat off, wiped the sweat from his brow with his forearm, and then situated the hat back on his curly head of dark hair. Tipping the brim up, he winked and said, "What's up, boss?"

I shrugged. "We need to talk." I should have started with an apology, but stubborn pride was a failing of mine, and I was going to take the long way around before I said I was sorry. "Come on up to the house and have some iced tea."

I turned and started back without waiting for his answer, but I felt his hesitation. He was stubborn, too, but then his long strides fell in step beside mine, and he was there before I was to hold the screen door open in his own courtly way.

We stomped our boots on the mat that lay just outside the kitchen door to shake off some of the dirt but it was a hopeless cause. Every day we tracked half the ranch into the kitchen and every night I swept it back out again. It was a battle I couldn't win, but I didn't know how to quit fighting.

Pete hung his hat on the rack by the back door, and then washed his hands at the sink while I poured the iced tea. He grabbed a lemon from the blue delft bowl on the table and sliced it into wedges. We sat at the table while the window unit hummed and rattled and put out enough cool air to make us feel human again. I sipped my tea, while he squeezed lemon into his. He drank his down in three long gulps, and when I got up to refill his glass he said, "The water pump on the Ford is shot. I'll pick up another one when I'm in town tomorrow."

"Are you going to town to see Sarah?" I tried to keep my tone neutral, but he bristled just the same.

"Andy has a baseball game, and I promised I'd be there, but don't worry. I'll still get my work done around here."

"I wasn't worried. And you certainly don't have to clear your plans with me, despite what I said this morning."

He sighed and fiddled with his glass. "I know I've been spending a lot of time in town, Goldie. And you have a right to expect me not to neglect things around here, but it's just until they get settled. Moving out here from Fort Worth has been rough on both of them."

"You've been a good friend, Pete." Sarah Powell might have been Pete's best friend's widow, but Brian had been gone for a while now, and it was beginning to look like Pete's interest went beyond friendship. The fact that she'd picked up and moved to Glenville with her eight-year-old son told me she probably felt the same. "She's lucky to have you."

"Brian was the lucky one. To have a family that loves you. That's the kind of thing that makes getting up every morning mean something."

3

Yep, he had it bad, and the longing in his voice was like an arrow lodged right in my heart. I swallowed something more sour tasting than pride and said, "I know I haven't been exactly understanding about all the time you've been taking off lately, but you've earned the right to negotiate your own terms around here. I apologize, and I want to make it up to you."

"You don't owe me anything, Goldie."

"The fact that you believe that is an insult, but we'll skip that part for now. Just let me finish, and if this is a bad idea, I'm sure you'll tell me."

"Sorry, boss." The grin on his face said he wasn't sorry at all. "Go ahead."

"As you know, summer is our busiest time of year, and if Sarah doesn't mind hard work, I could always use an extra hand. And Andy would have other kids to hang out with. I mean, it might be good for them to be busy and occupied..."

Pete stood up from his chair, his expression gone from cocky to solemn in no time. I trailed to a stop, not sure if he liked the idea or hated it.

Before I could blink he wrapped his arms around my waist and twirled me around the kitchen. When he set me back on my feet his brown eyes were shining, and he planted a big kiss on my cheek.

"Goldie Miller, underneath that thick-skinned, tough-talkin' exterior of yours, you're hiding a big-hearted, generous, magnificent woman, and I'll fight anyone who says otherwise." Looking like a man on a mission, he grabbed his hat and headed out the kitchen door. He paused at the threshold and turned back to face me. In a low, quiet voice he said, "You're one of kind, boss." Then he winked and ran for his truck.

"I guess you liked the idea," I said to his retreating pick-up as it pulled out toward town in a cloud of dust.

With a resigned sigh I turned my back on the window, and went to check the pot of beef stew that simmered on the stove. The rest of my crew would be hitting the back door soon, and they'd be hungry enough to eat anything that wasn't tied down, including my lousy cooking. If it wasn't beans, or chili, or stew, or some other concoction that could be thrown together in one pot, I

4

didn't tackle it. I'd just slid a batch of biscuits from the oven when I saw the men heading across the yard.

Jefferson Polk ambled into the kitchen, all lanky legs, swaggering smiles, and slicked-down blond hair. He must have stuck his head under the nearest water faucet to clean up and used his fingers for a comb. "Something in here almost smells good enough to eat, Goldie."

"Hush up and sit down, Jefferson, or I'll give you an extra helping."

He held up his hands in mock surrender. "I'm sittin'," he drawled before straddling a chair.

Bobby John Crawford stomped his boots on the mat outside the door and said, "Don't pay him any attention, ma'am. Your food's not that bad."

I laughed at the back-handed compliment. "Why thank you, Bobby John. Just for that I won't make you eat seconds. Go on, you sit, too. Everything's ready."

"Yes, ma'am," he said agreeably. Bobby was only twenty-two, young and strong and he worked as long as there was work to be done without complaining. I wished I could clone about a dozen of him, but instead I set a bowl of watery stew in front of him and added a couple of extra biscuits to his plate.

Warren Grimes strode in and hung his hat on the hook by the back door. "Evenin', Goldie."

"Evenin', Warren." He'd worked on the ranch for twenty-five years, longer than anybody except Pete. He was in his late forties, and his wife, Bertha, usually did the cooking, but she was gone to San Antonio to help their daughter with a complicated pregnancy and lend a hand with their other grandchild. He was very diplomatic about the food that was being served in her absence.

"I saw Pete headed toward town," he noted before joining the other two at the table.

"He's been doing that a lot lately." Jefferson waggled his eyebrows. "I do believe he's sweet on Sarah Powell."

I slapped bowls of stew in front of both of them a little harder than necessary. "Who Pete is sweet on is none of our business. And right now he's gone to offer her a job helping out here for the summer. Now eat your supper while it's hot."

They looked surprised, but didn't make any more

comments about Pete or Sarah. I sat down with them, pushing my food around the bowl with my spoon. I knew hiring Sarah had been my idea, but I still felt out of sorts and prickly about it, like having her at the ranch would upset the balance of things. And it probably would.

The guys ignored my bad temper and dug into their dinner. I half listened as they talked about the brush that needed to be cleared, the bunkhouse that needed painting and who was going to win the high school baseball game. Even as they went back for seconds they tried to get my goat by begging Warren to get Bertha back home as soon as he could, so she could take over the cooking duties again. I shook myself from my funk long enough to pretend to be insulted. I didn't want to ruin all their fun.

After the meal, they trooped out to finish up the evening chores. Once the summer camps started, Jefferson and Bobby John would spend the night in the bunkhouse, but for now they went home to their own places. Jefferson had a double-wide trailer on a small piece of land. Bobby John still lived with his parents in town, and Warren and Bertha had a house a few miles up the road.

I washed and dried the dishes while Pete's yellow rose taunted me from its perch on the windowsill. I draped the damp dish towel on the oven door handle to dry, and picked up the broom, attacking the kitchen floor like a fishwife going after her cheating husband. By the time I heard the men leave for the night, I was worn out and as broody as an old hen.

Even though it was still early I went around shutting off lights and locking doors. Thinking it might help to read, I went to my bedroom and pulled back the covers. After I showered, I slipped into my cotton nightgown and had barely settled under the covers with my book when I heard the sound of an engine as someone pulled into the yard. I looked out the window, surprised to see Pete's truck parked back by the barn. Without another thought, I grabbed my robe and went outside.

The night was still warm, but a nice breeze stirred the air as I let myself out of the house. Across the yard the barn loomed, hulking and dark except for the light spilling out of the open door. The dry grass was coarse and brittle under my bare feet, reminding me I should have grabbed my slippers before rushing out of the house like I had a fire to get to. But I threw back my shoulders and mulishly marched on toward the barn like going barefoot had been a deliberate fashion choice.

My long curly hair was unbraided and still a little damp from the shower. I batted it out of my eyes and pulled wayward strands from my mouth as it caught in the breeze and danced around my head like so many dark uncoiling snakes.

I didn't call out his name as I approached this time. I was big enough to admit that I was feeling pushed aside by Pete's interest in another woman. I was used to getting all his attention--well not me, but the ranch--and I was jealous. So I planned to waltz right in without announcing myself, and if he had a problem with that he could suck eggs.

My entrance only caused him to grin and give me the once over. "Why, Miss Goldie, are you trying to scare the livestock?"

The horses made snuffling noises from their stalls at the sound of his voice. I smoothed a hand over my unruly hair and pulled my robe around myself like armor. "I heard your truck and wanted to see how things went with Sarah." It wasn't as if he hadn't seen me in a nightgown before. Or with bare feet, or with my hair flying loose and wild, but the ease I'd always found around Pete had deserted me of late, and if I'd been standing in front of him buck naked I couldn't have felt more vulnerable.

He put down the lead he was holding and brightened at the mention of Sarah's name. "She'll come by tomorrow to iron out the details, but she's really grateful for the offer. Thanks again, Goldie."

"Glad I could help. Did you have dinner? I saved you some stew, just in case."

"Thanks, but I ate with Sarah and Andy. I just came by to finish up a few things. I didn't mean to drag you out of bed."

"Oh, I was just reading, and thinking."

"You always did think too much for your own good."

"Somebody around here has to. This place doesn't run itself."

"Don't go getting all riled up, Goldie. I'm just teasing."

The fight went out of me like water down a bathtub drain and I sat down on the nearest bale of hay. "Sorry. I don't know why I'm so touchy lately. It must be the drought. I nearly bit Jefferson's head off at supper."

"Jefferson probably deserved it. That boy's got a big mouth on him." He looked annoyed. "If he gets out of hand again you let me know, and I'll take care of it."

"The day I can't handle a smart-mouthed cowboy is the day I'll sell this place and move to the big city."

"Is that what you've been thinking about, Goldie?" His dark eyes bore into me like he was pondering the meaning of life. "You wouldn't really sell the place, would you?"

"If it doesn't rain, I won't have to. It'll just dry up and blow away into the next county."

"We need the rain, but you've gotten through worse times, and you'll weather this, too."

"Not without you, Pete." I blurted it out, sounding more desperate than I planned.

He sat down beside me and nudged me with his elbow. "Did you fire me and forget to tell me?"

"Of course not."

"Then what's this all about?"

"I've been thinking--"

"You mentioned that before." He grinned but then sobered up and put on his listening face. Growing up, I'd always bent his ear with my childish dramas, and even though he was five years older than me he never once acted like he couldn't be bothered. Whether it was because Laurie Dalton said I was ugly in front of the whole sixth grade math class, or because my dad wouldn't let me go to the junior high dance with Brad Kramer, he never made me feel like he was putting up with me because his dad worked for my dad. I always knew I could count on him to make me feel better, but I didn't have the same confidence that tonight's conversation would turn out that same way.

"Since Dad died you know how I've struggled to keep the ranch going. It's taken all my energy, and yours, too."

"You're dad would be proud."

That he thought so meant a lot, but I plunged on before I got sidetracked. "Have you ever thought about getting married?"

He stood up like he'd been popped from a toaster. "What in the Sam Hill made you ask that?"

"Don't worry. I'm not proposing. I've just been thinking that someone your age is probably looking to settle down and have kids, and as hard as you work around here, it probably puts a hitch in your love life."

"My love life is just fine, thank you." He crossed his arms and glared at me.

I lifted my chin and asked bluntly, "Because of Sarah?"

He eyed me warily. While we might have discussed my life at length over the years, who he dated and why had always been a subject that was off limits. He wasn't the kind to kiss and tell. "Sarah's a friend--a friend that needs help right now. I thought we straightened this out before I went to town."

"I'm not trying to stick my nose where it doesn't belong. I'm just trying to be more sensitive to your needs."

He let out a bark of laughter. "My needs? Just what do you know about my needs, little girl?"

I bristled at his implication. "I'm not a little girl, and in case you haven't noticed, I haven't been for a long time. All I'm trying to say is that if you want more time off--"

"To take care of my needs?" He stomped over to the work bench and turned his back on me.

"--I'll understand," I continued, ignoring the ache I felt at the thought of him marrying someone else. But if that was what he wanted, I'd give him my blessing.

"Go back to bed, Goldie."

He wouldn't look at me, so I got up and walked to the barn door. Sighing loudly I said, "I'm just trying to help. You're not getting any younger, you know."

I stomped off to bed not feeling the least bit better.

**

I was working in the garden early the next morning when I heard a car drive into the yard. I shaded my eyes and saw Sarah Powell getting out of a small blue car. Her pink sundress made a splash of color against the brown yard as she spotted me and made her way in my direction. I took off my gloves and went to meet her halfway.

I could see that she was small and delicate, pretty and feminine. Not like me. I'd always been a tomboy, tall and gangly but strong as an ox, and proud of it. Who had time for make-up and silly dresses when there was always so much work to be done? Keeping the ranch had been my sole responsibility from the time I was Bobby John's age, and I didn't know any other way. As I got closer I noticed the porcelain texture of her skin and the smooth blonde sweep of her hair. I smoothed my rough hands self-consciously down the front of my dirty overalls, and for the first time in my life being one of the boys didn't seem to be quite good enough.

"I'm Sarah," she said holding out her hand. We'd met once when her husband was still alive, but she probably didn't remember me.

"I'm Goldie. I guess you're here to talk about the job?" I shook her hand, sounding too brusque so I dredged up a smile.

Instead of letting my hand go, she grabbed on for dear life and started babbling ninety to nothing. "I can't tell you what this means to me. I'm a hard worker, and I'll do anything you ask." Her pale blue eyes filled with that combination of desperation and eagerness you only see in the eyes of a puppy seeking adoption at the pound. I'd planned on not liking her, just because she was taking up so much of Pete's time, but it was hopeless. I let her into my kitchen the same way I'd let in any stray that scratched at the back door.

I sat her at the table and put the kettle on for hot tea. Despite the summer heat, I still liked a civilized cup of tea with my mid-morning break. And she was as delicate as the china tea cups that belonged to my mother. I set a cup and saucer in front of her along with some defrosted banana nut muffins Bertha had mercifully left in the freezer. Then I sat down to interview my newest employee.

"So, Sarah, what kind of experience do you have?"

Her eyes widened and her face grew paler. "Experience?"

"Don't worry. I'm just trying to find your niche,

where you'd be the most useful."

"As I said, I'm a hard worker, and I'm willing to do anything." She was getting that desperate look again.

"Do you have any experience with horses?"

She shook her head.

"How about chickens or cows?"

She shook her head again.

"We plant a big garden to help feed the kids for camps."

"I managed to kill all the plants in my house in Fort Worth." She sounded defeated. "But I'm willing to learn."

I had a sudden brainstorm. "What about cooking?" After all, she had a son who required feeding, and Pete had mentioned eating with them the night before. If Bertha didn't make it home before the next camp started I'd have to find a temporary replacement for her anyway.

Her face lit up like life's greatest conundrum had been unraveled at last. "I can. In fact, I'm a good cook."

"That's settled then. For now, you'll be responsible for lunch and supper for the small crew I have working now." She looked like she might fall to the floor and kiss my dirty boots in gratitude, so I slapped the table and stood. "Once camp starts we bring in a camp cook, and the kids help prepare their own meals. You can be Cookie's assistant. Can you start tomorrow?"

"Of course. I'll be here bright and early."

"Pete told you Andy's welcome to attend the camps as part of your job, didn't he? Feel free to bring him along anytime."

"He told me." I thought she was going to start crying, so I grabbed our cups and set them in the sink to give her a minute to compose herself. Her voice sounded all watery. "Goldie, I don't know if you realize what this job means to me."

"Nonsense." I hoped crying wasn't going to be a daily thing, but she'd been through a lot, and I wasn't completely heartless. "I should be thanking you. If the boys had to eat my cooking much longer, I would have had a rebellion on my hands."

Just then Pete came in the back door. His hat was tipped back on his head and his brown eyes sparkled when he spotted her. She smiled like she'd just been named Miss America and ran and threw herself into his arms. "Hey, Pete, I'm the new cook."

He smiled even as he caught her and held her off. "Hold on there. You'll get your nice dress all dirty." He'd been out with Warren clearing the last of the brush from the riding trails, and he was covered in dirt and sweat.

"Who cares about a dress? I've got a job." She wouldn't be held off, and he finally gave in and let her hug his waist.

I tried not to notice how well they fit together, how his big hand spread protectively across her back or the way he smiled down at her like she was fragile and precious. And they sure didn't notice when I slipped out of the kitchen and into my office off the living room. I sat at my desk, trying not to feel pushed aside again. She was a lovely person, and I could tell she would do a good job or die trying. And Pete was happy to have her here. That was all that mattered.

"Where'd you get to, Goldie?" Pete was calling, and I couldn't keep hiding away like a scorned lover, so I got up and rejoined them in the kitchen.

Sarah grabbed my hand and gushed some more. "I better get back to town, but I'll be here first thing tomorrow. And I promise you won't be sorry."

After hugging Pete one more time, she left. He watched her drive off and said, "I'll be working on the truck if you need me."

"Aren't you going to make any smart remarks about not having to eat my cooking anymore?"

"I was just going to wait until I was out of sight and turn a few cartwheels." With a smirk, he headed out the door.

I threw a leftover biscuit at his head as he ducked out. It sounded like a rock hitting the door frame, and I could hear him laughing as he ambled across the yard toward the barn.

**

I'm a lousy cook. I admit it. But men can be so stupid. Just because Sarah made chicken and dumplings--excuse me--*homemade* chicken and dumplings--was no reason for everyone to act like they'd just been liberated from a POW camp where they'd been forced to survive on vermin and rice.

I was exhausted, the good kind of exhausted that comes from a hard day of physical labor. We'd been out dredging the swimming hole, and I looked like something the cat dragged in. Pete and I were discussing the low water levels when Sarah appeared at the back door wearing a yellow dress and a white frilly apron, for pity's sake. Andy was all spiffed up, and he ran and wrapped himself around Pete's leg as soon as he saw him.

"Go get washed up, boys. Supper's ready," Sarah called merrily. "And Andy, leave Pete alone."

When he didn't let go, Pete swooped the boy into the air. "Mind your mama, kiddo. I'll be in after I clean up, okay?"

Andy nodded shyly and ran back to Sarah. They seemed like the perfect family and my disposition darkened. Jefferson and Bobby John tripped over each other trying to get to the bunkhouse first. Warren and Pete didn't behave that foolishly, at least not while I was watching. I rolled my eyes and retreated to my bedroom.

Stripping off my dirty clothes, I stepped under the shower to wash off the top layer of dirt and threw on some old sweats. Then I picked a few pieces of grass from my hair, before going to the kitchen. It was empty, but the sound of happy cowboys drifted in from the seldom-used formal dining room.

I walked in, taking in the fancy place mats and the good china. My ranch hands had never looked so clean or smelled so sweet. Bobby John must have used up a whole bottle of cologne. And the way they vied for Sarah's attention. She filled a plate here and passed a bowl there, smiling and happy. And if they weren't all in hog heaven, I don't know where pork goes to die.

When I sat down in a chair next to Pete, he reached over and pulled a twig from my hair. "Missed something," he said.

"Thanks," I said jerking the corners of my mouth up in a poor imitation of a smile.

Jefferson had done more than stick his head under the faucet tonight. Besides his clean shirt, he sported a bolo tie complete with a silver spur slide. And it looked like he'd actually used a comb, too. "Sarah," he said, "you better sit down now and eat while the food's hot."

"Yeah, sit." Warren insisted. "Ma'am, this is sure good."

Before I could reach for the tureen, Sarah was there waiting on me. She filled my bowl with thick chicken and dumplings and my mouth watered at the aroma. She added yeast rolls so light they almost floated above my plate and fresh green beans. Then she finally sat down and filled her own plate. Pete had taken care of Andy, and both of them were happily stuffing their faces.

I took a bite and almost moaned it was so good. Sarah was watching, anxious for my reaction. "It's delicious," I said. Her whole body lit up when she smiled and every man in the room seemed to fall just a little bit more in love with her.

I ate every bite on my plate, listening to Pete and Andy talk about his baseball game. Andy had gotten a hit and scored a run, and Pete was saying they could toss the ball around some night after dinner. I was about to go back for seconds, but Sarah went to the kitchen and came back with a huge banana pudding. I thought the men might weep at the sight.

Bobby John picked up his spoon and tapped it on his water glass. "I'd like to make a toast." We all waited patiently. "To Miss Goldie, for hiring Miss Sarah, so we don't have to eat her cooking anymore."

Everyone turned wide eyes in my direction, not sure what my reaction would be. Poor Bobby John was starting to turn a bright shade of red, so I decided to let him off the hook. I raised my glass and said, "So what if I can't cook? I sure know how to hire 'em. To Sarah. Welcome to the Double M family, and you too, Andy." I winked at the boy who still seemed unsure of me.

Everyone relaxed then and forgot about everything but getting their share of banana pudding. Pete leaned over and whispered, "You're a good sport, Goldie."

I don't know why that made me want to cry. I don't do tears. I'm stoic, unemotional, detached even, but Pete's verbal equivalent of a pat on the back made me want to run outside and howl at the moon. I didn't want to keep a stiff upper lip. I didn't want to keep my cool. I didn't want to pretend that every time Pete smiled at Sarah some deep wound inside me didn't tear open a little wider.

I couldn't bear to stay in the house any longer, so after a few bites of dessert I excused myself, slipped out to the front porch, and curled up on the old wooden glider. My mama and dad spent many an evening on that old thing, and I'd caught them kissing on it a time or two.

I don't know how long I sat, barely aware of the sounds inside the house as supper finished up and the table was cleared. I absently noted the voices of the men and Sarah calling out goodbyes as they headed home, then watched their headlights sweep across the road before disappearing into the night.

I pushed myself back and forth with one foot, searching for the moon in the deep purple sky. A sound like June bugs hitting a screen made me sit up. My mother's yellow rose bush grew next to the porch and I realized the sound was raindrops hitting the leaves. Even in the twilight I could see the drops glistening on the yellow petals. I shouted the only name that mattered. "Pete."

I walked into the yard, letting the driving rain hit my upturned face. The sky opened, drenching the parched earth beneath my feet, soaking my clothes, washing away my last defenses. Tears ran down my face and I cried, for the ranch I'd fought so hard to keep. I cried for Pete, the boy I'd always loved, and for the man I needed still. "Pete." I said his name softly this time, and like an answered prayer he was there, shouting my name, wrapping me in his arms. Kissing me.

"It's raining, Goldie." Lightening lit up the sky, and he kissed me again, just like he did it every day of his life.

I was still crying like a big baby. "Don't kiss me if you love Sarah. I can't bear it. I'll sell you the ranch and move away, and you'll never have to see me again."

He shushed me with another kiss. "What good would this old place be without you?" He picked me up like I didn't weigh a thing and carried me to the glider. Sitting down with me on his lap he said, "I've been thinking."

"I thought that was my job," I blubbered.

"It is, but you've been doing it all wrong lately." He cupped my cheek in his hand and wiped away my tears with his thumb.

I sat up straighter and sniffed. "Is that so?"

"That's so. You keep trying to marry me off to Sarah, and everyone knows I'm in love with you."

"Since when?" My heart thundered at his words.

"Since I've been helping her with the move. You've got this idea in your head that we make some perfect couple."

He deliberately misunderstood my question, but I still had to try to make my case. "Sarah's beautiful."

He nodded his head and agreed, "She's gorgeous."

I glared. "She's delicate and wears frilly aprons."

"Keep going," he said. "Maybe you can still convince me."

I sat poker straight on his lap when all I wanted to do was melt against him. "Since when?" I repeated forlornly. "Since when have you been in love with me?"

He seemed to consider the question while tucking a wet curl behind my ear. "I guess I've loved you in some fashion all my life, but after your daddy died, I watched you grow from a headstrong little girl into a tough, beautiful woman who, come hell or high water, fought for what was hers. I wanted to be someone you thought was worth fighting for, Goldie."

"Oh, Pete." When I said his name this time my voice trembled with wonder. "Don't you know how much I love you? If you're not by my side nothing else matters much, not even the Double M."

I leaned in touching my lips to his. He tasted of coffee, and longing, and home, sweet, home. Then his mouth grew hot and hungry, like the wind howling through the mesquite trees. His strong arms held me, sheltering me from the pouring rain. I wrapped my arms around his neck, openly claiming him as my own, and thought of long nights and four poster beds...and Pete.

About the Author

I was born and raised in Texas and grew up reading everything I could get my hands on. Reading was my first true love. But then I met my husband Bill and books took a back seat. We got married and raised three wonderful children. Now that they're grown and gone, I spend my time running an adult soccer league and writing stories of mystery and romance. My website is www.martytidwell.com

Wallflowers

by

Marty Tidwell

Dedication

This is for my sisters Sherri and Patti,
for my sisters at the HB, and for anyone else
who's ever had an unlikely crush.

"You're Rory Cooper." The words fell out of her mouth, a startled accusation, hanging in the air between her and the man standing behind the cash register at Petal Pusher's Garden Shop. His name tag might say Michael J. Bankins, but that didn't do anything to change her mind about his identity.

She'd just lifted a flat of yellow petunias from her cart and set it down on the counter to pay when she found herself staring into his familiar face. The blond hair was darker, the blue eyes more worldly, and the face fifteen years older, but it was still a face she knew as well as she knew her own.

He glanced at the people in line behind her, and without acknowledging her claim, asked instead, "Did you find everything you were looking for, ma'am?"

Well now. That all depended.

When she'd shown up for the grand opening of Merlington's newest garden shop, she'd been looking for purple petunias, but the yellow blossoms had flirted shamelessly, convincing her to buy them instead. She had a weakness for yellow, and despite her yearly resolution to branch out and plant a different color of flower around the trees in the front yard, somehow she always came home with something yellow. This year it was petunias.

What else had she been looking for?

She certainly hadn't been looking for Rory Cooper. But here he was, right in front of her.

He moved around the counter with his bar-code reader in his hand and scanned the prices on the remaining flats stacked on her cart. "Will that be all?" He looked at her then, and smiled the smile she remembered from all those years before.

"You're Rory Cooper," she repeated a little more insistently.

The smile faded from his eyes, and with another glance at his other customers he introduced himself. "The name's Michael Bankins, ma'am. I'm the new owner of this place, and I'm afraid you have me confused with someone else."

"Not unless you have a twin brother," she stated bluntly.

"I'm an only child." His tone was polite, but brusque, and he paused with his hand above the keys of the register ready to total up her purchases. "Will this be all for you today?" The look in his eyes seemed to suggest that the subject was closed for good.

She studied his face, not convinced in the least that she'd made such a mistake, but the line of people behind her was getting longer, and so for now, she pretended to concede. "Yes, that'll be all, thanks." She handed him her credit card and while he swiped it through his machine she said, "Welcome to town, Michael Bankins." She waved her hand around at the large nursery. He'd taken the old, run-down garden center and turned it into a magical place. Winding paths filled with plants and trees, flowers and vines, benches and birdbaths, were designed to make the customers want to buy it all and transform their own yards into something magical, too. "You've done wonders with this place. And by the way, I'm not usually so rude."

With his real smile back in place, he read her name from the credit card before returning it to her with her receipt. "No problem, Ms. Stafford. Enjoy the flowers, and come back anytime."

"Thanks. I will." She pushed her cart toward the exit gate glancing back repeatedly to steal furtive glimpses of the man before heading for her car. Her heart was rocketing around madly in her chest as she wondered where in the world he'd been all this time.

She hadn't seen him in fifteen years. He'd been her first love, her first adolescent crush. Rory Cooper, star of Rompin' Rodeo, a regional kid's show broadcast out of Dallas. It was aimed at younger children, but after catching a glimpse of the cute teenager one afternoon while switching channels, she'd become a devoted viewer. He was the young fresh-faced sidekick to the older host, Cowboy Dan. They wore ten-gallon hats and fancy cowboy boots with silver spurs, crisp western shirts with pearly snaps. They told corny jokes, and introduced cartoons, and she should have thought he was the dorkiest guy around. The boys she knew wouldn't have been caught dead wearing that slick western get up.

But during every show came the moment Ellie waited for all day long. Cowboy Dan would look at Rory and say, "How about a song, son?" And Rory would pick up his guitar, strum it with his long dancing fingers, and he'd sing.

And she was sure he was singing just to her.

Her thirteen-year-old heart would melt as he warbled and yodeled and yippee-yi-yo-ki-ayed his way through a country song. The camera would move in, do a close up on his face, and those sincere blue eyes of his would bore right through her television set and into her soul.

She'd sent off to the television station for his autographed posters and tacked them up all over her bedroom walls. And when her door was closed at night, before she went to sleep, she would tell him her trials and troubles, whisper her longed-for wishes, and confide her deepest desires.

Even though her mother teased her about her obsession, she also told her it must run in the family. She said she'd been a Beatle-maniac in her youth, and her Grandma Dee had been crazy about Elvis, making yearly trips to Vegas to see him in his later years.

Ellie was embarrassed to have her feelings trivialized and didn't consider it to be the same thing at all, but she continued to watch him faithfully every day after school and dream about him faithfully every night.

Then it happened.

She came home and turned on the television to find he'd been replaced by little Jimmy Shelton. Little Jimmy Shelton! The guy was cute, and he could sing, but he was about ten years old, for Pete's sake, and he wasn't Rory.

She never watched the show again. She did write to the station to find out if they could tell her where he'd gone or why he'd left, but they just wrote back saying he was no longer with the show. He was lost to her, vanished without a trace, and even though her adolescent heart was broken, it soon healed, as adolescent hearts do. Still, Rory's posters stayed on her walls until she left home to go to college.

She hadn't thought about him for years. Naturally,

her life had gone on, and there had been real boys to date in high school, and as she got older, a few good men who'd captured her affection. Not recently, however. Sad to say, she hadn't had a good rousing romance since she'd moved back to Merlington to take care of her mother.

Seeing Rory had been a jolting reminder of a lonesome time in her life, a time he'd helped her get through. Of course, he had no way of knowing that, but she still wondered why he seemed so intent on denying his past. She realized it was a question that would probably never be answered.

So, when he showed up at her house a few days later, she was caught off guard. "Mornin', Ms. Stafford."

"Mornin', Mr. Bankins." She was wearing her usual work clothes, a pair of ancient stained jeans and an old t-shirt that was a few years past being ready for the rag bag. Her brown hair was caught back in a half-hearted pony tail and covered with a red bandana. Throwing pots was a messy business, and she dressed accordingly. Entertaining company clearly hadn't been on her list of things to do.

At least he couldn't know how her heart did a hop, skip and a jump when she'd opened her front door to find him standing there. She tried not to gawk, but it was like opening her door and finding out that Elvis had come to call on Grandma Dee.

Except he wasn't wearing a flashy sequined jump suit. But just the same, the plain working-man jeans covering his long legs and the clean white shirt stretching over his wide chest made her want to squeal like a groupie. His straight blond hair fell across his forehead in ways that made her fingers itch, and his eyes were bluer than any pair of blue suede shoes Elvis ever thought of singing about.

But her steady voice never betrayed her fluttering emotions when she asked, "Did you come to make sure I planted my petunias properly?"

He glanced behind him at the newly installed profusion of flowers surrounding the trees in her front yard before turning mocking blue eyes back her way. "We do like to make sure our plants go to good homes." He shuffled his feet a little and seemed unsure when he held out a single yellow rose. "And I brought a peace offering."

She accepted the flower and held it to her nose. It smelled divine, but she was suspicious by nature and in her experience, an unexpected man bearing a flower usually had an agenda that merited close scrutiny. She eyeballed the divine-looking man filling up her front porch and said as if she smelled something fishy, "I didn't know we were at war."

He shrugged. "I was a little short with you the other day at the nursery, and since I'm just getting started, I can't afford to run away potential customers."

She didn't buy that charming load of cow manure for one minute, but since she still had lots of unanswered questions, she pushed open the screen door and asked, "In that case would you like some coffee? We can drink it on the back patio, and you can make sure my other potted plants haven't been abused."

He followed her through the house and into the kitchen. On the chance that he might be hungry, she grabbed a serving tray and filled it with coffee and homemade muffins. Sticking the yellow rose in a bud vase, she added it to the tray as a finishing touch and led him out to the backyard.

She watched him pause to scan the landscaped yard. Flower-filled ceramic pots in varying colors and finishes lined the patio and sat scattered among the trees and flower beds. He walked around examining them with great interest.

"So, what's this visit really about, Mr. Bankins?" She poured the coffee and waved him into a chair.

"Please, call me Michael." And not Rory, his eyes seemed to add. He'd always had the most expressive eyes.

"Okay, Michael. I'm Ellie." She sipped her coffee and tried to wait patiently while he helped himself to a blueberry muffin.

"These look great. I skipped breakfast this morning."

She watched him take a bite and felt like pinching herself. Or maybe she should get up and pinch him instead to see if he was real. No matter what he was calling himself these days, Rory Cooper was sitting on her patio not three feet away. It was the last thing she ever expected. If a space ship landed right now and twenty-five little green men marched out and crowned her Queen of Mars she wouldn't blink an eye. Not with Rory Cooper eating a cotton pickin' blueberry muffin in her backyard. Talk about your wildest dreams.

Finally he swallowed and said, "I know who you are, Ellie. I did some digging around and asked about you. People around here don't seem to mind sharing information with strangers."

"This is a friendly place. Why don't you tell me what they said so I can defend myself?"

"Well, let's see. You grew up right here in Merlington--right here in this house, as a matter of fact. Went away somewhere back east to college, and then lived in Dallas for a while. Moved back when your mother got sick, and then after she died, you decided to stay. Oh, and you have a ceramic studio in town, and your work can be found in shops and galleries all around Texas."

"I don't think you got that last part from talking to the people in town. They think I spend all my time teaching kids how to make coffee mugs to give to their moms for birthday presents."

He picked up the mug he'd been drinking from and examined it. The cup was lopsided and the handle was attached at an odd angle. "Is this one of yours?"

She laughed. "One of my first. It took me a while to get the knack of pulling handles, but still, it's one of my favorites."

He tilted his head and said, "It has character."

"Thank you, I think."

"And that's why I'm here. I'd like to commission some work from you."

"Really? Based on that mug?" She put her hands on her hips and didn't try to hide her skepticism.

He stood up and walked over to one of the large pots that surrounded the edge of the patio. "I assume this is one of yours, too." He squatted down and ran his hand across the metallic-looking green surface of a large Raku pot filled with red geraniums. "It's beautiful."

"It's one of mine, but I saw stacks and stacks of every size and style of planter imaginable at your store yesterday, Michael. Why would you need mine?"

"Because these are works of art, Ellie." He stood up

and faced her. "I sometimes do projects that need something above and beyond the mass-produced pots and planters I sell in the nursery. I'm in the process of putting together a group of local artisans I can call on for various projects. If you're interested, you can stop by the shop later, and I can show you the plans of some of the projects I've done recently."

She could use the extra money, but still, she suspected his motives. "I'm always interested in getting more exposure for my work, but why me? I'm wondering if this has more to do with our first encounter than it does with you being impressed by my pottery."

Those blue eyes were boring into her, snagging her soul in that old, yet still familiar way. "I set high standards, Ms. Stafford, and your work was recommended by people I trust. If I didn't think you could bring something special to the group, I wouldn't be here."

No matter what kind of soul-stirring this man was capable of, she'd be foolish to fall for his flattery. "Maybe this is just your way of bribing me to keep quiet?"

"There's nothing to keep quiet about." His eyes softened, and his voice slid over her, smooth as butterscotch pudding, a deeper echo of the adolescent voice she remembered so well. "I thought we settled that, Ellie." Hearing him say her name made her restless, cut adrift from the here and now, until his next question pulled her back down to earth. "So, would you be interested? Tell me you'll at least think about it." He added his smile to the mix, beguiling her, coaxing her, as if all she needed was a little persuading.

But still she managed to hold back, resisting the temptation to be so easily charmed without getting a few answers first. "I'd be dumb not to consider your offer, but why don't you tell me more about yourself before I make a decision? Where are you from originally?"

"I grew up in East Texas, in a small town right outside of Tyler."

"The rose capital of Texas? Is that why you're into plants now?"

"I'm afraid not. I couldn't tell one green thing from another until I was in college and went to work in a nursery to help pay my way through school. I liked it so much I changed my major, and the rest is history."

"What about when you were a teenager? Did you ever live in Dallas?" No one would ever accuse her of being subtle.

He laughed, but before he could come up with a new way to avoid answering, the pager on his belt buzzed. He glanced down, read the message, and then crossed the patio until he was standing close enough to touch. "I'm sorry, but I've got a job to go bid on right now. Why don't we meet later this afternoon at the nursery, if that's okay? And I'll answer all your questions then."

"All of them?" she asked with wide-eyed innocence, but they both knew her questions weren't just about the job. "I'll have my list ready."

"You do that, Ellie." And there it was again, her name on his lips, while his eyes flickered with some dangerous combination of challenge, warning and invitation. "Does four o'clock work for you?"

She walked with him toward the back gate and agreed at least to the meeting. "Four will do just fine."

He grinned like he'd won first prize in a pie-eating contest and gave her a friendly pat on the back. "That's great. I'll see you then."

She stood watching him walk away, watched as those long-as-a-country-mile legs carried him across her front yard, watched as he climbed into his pick-up truck and started the engine. And she was still watching when he blessed her with one last grin and a final wave before driving away. Then she turned like a woman on a mission and marched inside her house.

Climbing up into her musty attic wasn't one of her favorite things to do, and she hadn't been up there since her mother died. Ignoring the hanging cobwebs, suspicious rustling noises and shadows that loomed in every corner, she shook off the case of heebie-jeebies that danced up and down her spine as she worked her way through stacks of discarded furniture and forgotten treasures.

So much of her life had been packed up and stored away in that stale, dusty space. The residue of her childhood dreams, the remnants of the life she'd made for herself in Dallas before her mother got sick, and finally the stitched-together existence she'd shared with her mother in her final days. Boxed up, taped up, and tucked away out of sight.

Michael was wrong about at least one thing. She hadn't decided to stay in Merlington after her mother died. She'd just never made the decision to leave again, and that wasn't the same thing at all. She'd buried herself in her pottery, filling the house and the yard with pieces of herself, empty vessels, formed out of clay and fired to hold their shape. She'd floated along day to day, focusing on her work, simply existing inside the empty walls of her childhood home. And somehow along the way, she'd allowed the rest of her life to fall by the wayside.

Seeing Rory again dislodged something that had been hiding deep inside her body, something that felt like expectation. For the first time in ages, it pumped through her arteries: an eagerness, a yearning, a wish. She wanted to embrace it, hold the feeling close, but it was like trying to hug smoke, illusive and fleeting.

Wrestling an old dresser out of the way, she finally spied the pile of cardboard boxes she'd been searching for nestled under one of the rafters. Clearing a path she pulled and pushed them over to the attic entrance and carried them down into the den. Sitting cross-legged on the floor she started digging through them. She had some things she wanted to find before four o'clock rolled around.

He wasn't anywhere to be found at four o'clock. She wandered into Petal Pusher's right on time, feeling a bit obvious for changing into a summer dress instead of leaving on the jeans and ratty t-shirt he'd seen her in earlier. But this was a business meeting, after all, and she'd persuaded herself that it was only right to spruce herself up a little, the way she would for any other business meeting. That didn't explain why she'd chosen the most feminine thing hanging in her closet, the yellow sundress that made her feel pretty and a little bit saucy, to boot. The form-fitting bodice clung to her curves, while the full skirt, if she turned just so, swirled about in a very un-business like manner. Face it. She was loaded for bear.

Maybe she needed extra ammunition while she faced this reincarnation of Rory Cooper. In reality, Michael

Bankins was a complete stranger to her. And yet, just the sight of him turned her insides sweet and mushy, like orange marmalade. The familiar sound of his voice made her pulse take flight. And when he aimed those big blue eyes in her direction, she dissolved like a spoonful of sugar stirred into a cup of hot tea.

All because of what he'd meant to her in the past.

It carried over, and as hard as she tried, she couldn't separate her feelings for that boy from the man he'd become. This was a lopsided encounter where he had advantages he didn't even know about.

So if she wanted to wear a yellow dress, and maybe look a little less like the pig farmer's wife she'd resembled the first two times he's seen her, she would.

"Are you Ellie Stafford?" a young woman wearing a Petal Pusher apron asked. At her nod the young woman continued. "Mr. Bankins is waiting for you in his office. Just follow that path past the gazebo, and you'll see it."

Ellie thanked her, adjusted the strap of her portfolio more securely onto her shoulder and started down the path, noticing once again the fairytale feel of the place. It was like entering a green wonderland of twinkling lights and fragrant blossoms. She wouldn't have been surprised if birds, squirrels and friendly white mice appeared to show her the way. She'd just passed the gazebo when a door opened and Michael stepped outside. She smiled and kept walking toward him even as her traitorous insides did that quivering jelly thing again.

"Good, you're here." He'd changed his clothes, too. Black slacks, black dress shirt, both suitable for a business meeting, or for keeping a woman off balance. "I'm sorry I wasn't out front to meet you."

"That's okay." She looked around and said inanely, "I really love what you've done with this place."

"I'll take that as a hopeful sign." He held open the door and escorted her to a drafting table that occupied a corner of the office. Taking her portfolio he set it aside before helping her up onto one of the two stools in front of a display. He moved a stack of gardening books aside and arranged some photographs in front of her. "Prepare to be wooed." His seductive voice was half promise, half dare.

She stuck out her chin and said bravely, "Woo away."

His expression as he started speaking was so earnest that she resisted the urge to reach over and smooth the worry lines from his brow. Instead she folded her hands in her lap and concentrated on what he had to say.

"I love this nursery," he said simply. "For me it's a dream come true, and becoming an important part of this community is something I hope to accomplish over the next few years. I want to put down solid roots." He laughed and shrugged self-consciously at the pun. "Make this place my home."

"That sounds nice." The idea that he would be around long-term settled inside her like a bird coming home to nest.

"Besides selling plants to anyone who walks in off the street, I've done a few small projects designing green spaces: a few pocket parks, some atriums, and some larger, individual estates." His enthusiasm started seeping into his words as he pointed to the photos that showed examples of his work. "I want to develop partnerships with local artisans for developing those finishing touches that will make my projects unique. I've already introduced myself to a local blacksmith and a decorative metal worker, and a couple of mosaic artists. I have a list of painters and a sculptor I want to talk to, and there's a glass blower over in the next county that sounds promising.

"But back to your work, Ellie. It's strong, and beautiful and graceful, and I'd be honored if you'd consider my offer, if it sounds like something you'd like to be a part of."

From the first glimpse, she was enchanted. She poured over the pictures and recognized the same magical quality that filled the nursery outside. She studied the list of people he was assembling, recognizing several local names whose work she admired.

He sat on the stool next to her, exuding an air of pride in his work, mixed with his own particular brand of masculine heat. And yet, she could also sense a certain anxious vulnerability that she found endearing. Finally, she looked over at him and said, "These are wonderful. I'd be foolish to say no."

He let out a deep breath and asked, "So, that's a

yes?"

"Let's call it a strong probably. I still have a few unanswered questions."

"Of course you do." He swiveled toward her and crossed his arms across his chest. "Did you bring your list?"

"I've already asked this, but I have to ask again. Why me? Most artists would kill their granddaddy and the mule he rode in on for a chance to be included in a group like this, and yet you come to me with an offer out of the blue. I know I do good work, but I'm also not the best-known ceramic artist in the area. Tell me that this offer isn't a direct result of our first meeting."

"The meeting where you accused me of being Rory Cooper?

"I see you remember the name."

"It's not a name I'm likely to forget. That day you came into the nursery got my attention, and so I checked you out. But I'm very selective about the people I work with, and it would take more than the threat of having my former life as a teenaged cowboy/singing star revealed to change that."

"So, I'm not crazy? You are him, or he's you. You're Rory Cooper?"

"It's embarrassing, but yes. For a few months I was Rory Cooper on TV."

"Why is that embarrassing?"

"Are you kidding? Do you remember the outfit I had to wear? And those songs I had to sing? We'd just moved to Dallas, and I was the new kid, trying to fit in, and you can't imagine how much I got teased at high school by the other kids."

She'd never considered what it might be like for him. "Was it really so awful?"

"Only when I'd be hanging out at the mall with my friends and a group of giggling ten-year-old girls would come up and ask for my autograph."

"I think that's sweet. The other kids were probably just jealous. You were quite a heartthrob, you know."

"A heartthrob?" He groaned. "Please. And you have the nerve to ask why it was embarrassing."

"So, if you hated it so much, why did you do it?"

"I got roped into it by my mother. She was dating Cowboy Dan at the time. I assume you remember Cowboy Dan?"

"And his trusty horse, Tulip. Who could forget Cowboy Dan?"

"Anyway, she convinced him to put me on the show. I think she thought if we were under foot all the time, he'd eventually ask her to marry him. But he didn't, and so one day they had an argument about it, and the next day we left town. That was the beginning and end of my career in show business."

"That must have been hard, leaving school, leaving all your friends behind."

"I was used to it. That wasn't the first or the last time Mom picked up and moved because of a man."

"And so now, you'd just as soon act as if it never happened?"

"It rarely comes up, believe me. I'm sure you're one of the few people who even remember that show. I wasn't trying to be mysterious, but it wasn't the happiest time in my life, and I hoped you'd eventually drop it. Why are you so interested in whether or not I was Rory Cooper?"

"Well, now it's my turn to be embarrassed."

"About what?"

She shrugged. "Maybe I wasn't that much different from those giggling little girls that asked for your autograph."

He seemed surprised, and then just as quickly, amused by the possibility. "Were you?"

"Well, I never saw you at the mall, and if I had, I would have been too shy to ask for an autograph, but..." Her words trailed off.

"But what?" His piercing blue eyes made it clear that he had no intention of letting her off the hook without a full explanation.

With a sigh she got down from the stool and grabbed her portfolio. "Let me show you something." Pulling out a rolled tube of paper sticking out of the top, she brought it over to the drafting table. She uncoiled the poster of the young man who'd graced her bedroom walls for all those years, and spread it out on the table in front of him. "I was going to confront you with this evidence if you refused to come clean about your former life."

He didn't say anything at first, just traced a finger over the autograph that said, 'To Ellie, Keep on Rompin', Rory'. He finally looked up and laughed. "I can't believe you have this."

"Oh, there's more where that came from. Your pictures were plastered all over my bedroom. I was such a big fan."

"Really?" His earlier embarrassment evaporated as everything male in him preened at the idea. "A big fan of mine?"

She quickly corrected him. "A big fan of Rory Cooper's."

"What's the difference?"

"Well, you made it clear that you're Michael Bankins, and I don't know whether I'm a fan of his yet or not." She realized she was swaying flirtatiously, making her skirt do that swirling around her legs thing so she hopped back up on the stool.

"Fair enough," he conceded. "Would it help if I yodeled?"

"You can make fun of me later, but first let me finish telling you about the crush I had on Rory."

"I'm not making fun of you, Ellie. Go ahead." With the lightest touch he brushed her hand with his. "I'm listening."

"I was thirteen the year my father died, the year my mother started working two jobs and was never home anymore. It may sound silly, but Rory was there for me every afternoon. For a while the house didn't seem so empty, and I didn't feel so alone because of him." She paused and then added, "Because of you."

"I think you're giving me too much credit. It was just a dumb kid's show." He seemed embarrassed again. Pushing away from the desk, he stood and paced a few feet away from her.

"That dumb kid's show made my life bearable, Michael. Rory Cooper was pretty special to me, and I can't have anyone saying anything bad about him, not even you." She scolded him, then added teasingly to lighten the mood, "Of course, he did break my heart when he left the show so suddenly."

He turned back in her direction, and allowed the ghost of a smile to haunt his face. "See, he didn't deserve your devotion after all."

"I wrote to the station, but they didn't say where you'd gone."

He drifted back to the stool, and sat down, while his voice took on a melancholy tone. "We used to pick up and move for the flimsiest of reasons. I'd just be settling into a different house in a new neighborhood, with a new school and new friends and then something would set my mom off--a fight with a boyfriend, or a customer that didn't leave a big enough tip, or a change in the season, and off we'd go again. She was so restless. In four years I went to seven different high schools. Not really long enough to make much of an impression anywhere."

Without thinking she reached out and touched his cheek, brushing a wayward strand of hair from his brow, giving comfort to the lonely boy that still lived somewhere inside the man. "Well, you made an impression on me."

The idea still seemed to astonish him. "I guess I did, didn't I?" He captured her hand, bringing her palm to his lips for a chaste kiss. "I'm beginning to think Rory was a pretty lucky guy."

"Just your luck, you moved to the same town where his number one crazy fan lives."

"Just my luck, his number one crazy fan has helped me understand some things from my past in a different way."

"I'm glad then. So what happened to your mom?"

He grinned, his affection for her clear. "She's living happily on a ranch in Oklahoma with husband number five."

"So, she finally found a place to stick?"

"In her case, I think it was finding the right person more than the right place. Cowboy Dan finally asked her to marry him, and they've been together for the last ten years."

"Oh, I love happy endings. What happened to Tulip?"

"Tulip died of old age. Her daughter, Daffodil, rules the roost now."

Ellie scrutinized the man beside her, seeing him with different eyes then when she'd first recognized him behind the counter at Petal Pushers. For the first time in years she felt unstuck, set loose from the limbo she'd languished in since her mother's death. A white-water rush of anticipation carried her toward the future as she said, "By the way, the answer's yes."

His bluer-than-blue eyes examined her curiously, and his pale yellow hair fell carelessly upon his brow. With a golden laugh that skipped around the room and wrapped her up in joy, he confessed, "I'm sorry, but I think I've forgotten the question."

"The job offer. If it still stands, I'd be happy to make the pots while you fill them with flowers and pretty green-growy things."

"Do you mean it, Ellie? I think that calls for a celebration, don't you? Why don't I take you to dinner?"

Letting her skirt swirl and settle around her, she stood up and said, "The answer is yes to all those questions, too."

She could think of a million other questions he might ask in the future, and a million reasons why she'd want to keep saying yes. But she didn't know this man, not really. He was a mystery wrapped in Rory Cooper's skin, more solid than a dream, less familiar than a long lost friend, and for the most part still unknown. But she knew one thing for certain. Getting to know him would be anything but boring.

After all, he had offered to yodel.

About the Author

I was born and raised in Texas and grew up reading everything I could get my hands on. Reading was my first true love. But then I met my husband Bill and books took a back seat. We got married and raised three wonderful children. Now that they're grown and gone, I spend my time running an adult soccer league and writing stories of mystery and romance. My website is www.martytidwell.com

The Double-Dog-Dare Dance

by

Nancy Connally

Dedication

To my real-life romance hero, Greg.

Sunny had never been to Boot Scootin' Bliss and Roadside Grill. After all, who wanted to venture inside a ramshackle building that had a rotating, oversized armadillo on the roof? Just because Debbie, Jan, and Troy—along with their two husbands and one wife—had morphed into Friday night regulars at the place didn't mean Sunny had to join them. But for the last month or so, every Thursday at work, they ambled up to Sunny's desk and tried to shame her into going. Debbie said she didn't get out enough. Jan worried that she would forget how to dance. And Troy was determined for her to meet his pal, Jake.

"Honest," Debbie said. "You'll love BSBARG."

The Tenacious Trio had taken to calling the Parker County dance place that after they'd bought black T-shirts with BSBARG emblazoned in reflective silver letters across the chest. The logo of a dancing couple—a hamburger and a bottle of beer, both wearing cowboy hats and cowboy boots—dominated the center of the T-shirt.

Eewwww!

About to decline the invitation yet again, Sunny tensed when Troy folded his arms across his chest and said, "I double-dog-dare you."

Not just a dare. A double-dog-dare. Sunny snatched the shirt from Debbie, told Troy to have this Jake Shane guy call her, and vowed she would not wear the poorly designed shirt tomorrow night no matter how big a discount she might get on food.

Jake Shane, indeed. He'd obviously changed his name in hopes of sounding more cowboy. Heaven help her.

****

The telephone jangled Sunny's world that evening as she cuddled into the corner of her living room sofa with the latest Tony Hillerman book. Wondering, as did Joe Leaphorn, whether a cherry on a piece of cake he'd been given could be poisonous, she picked up the receiver and checked the Caller ID.

Hmm... Unknown Caller. She promptly stuffed the receiver between the cushions but Unknown Caller stayed on the line during the answering machine's greeting. After the beep a non-recorded baritone voice muttered, "This is a joke, isn't it? Man, I knew Troy was pulling my leg. Nobody's really named Sunny Climes—"

Sunny grabbed the phone. "It is Sunny Cleh-*mez* for your information." Only then did she stop to realize she didn't know who she was talking to. Although, given he'd mentioned Troy, she had a good idea.

"Where'd you get a name like Sunny Cleh-*mez*?" the man asked.

"My parents." She played her hunch. "When did you change yours to Jake Shane?"

"When I found out no one knew how to spell Karamazov."

He'd read Dostoevsky's *The Brothers Karamazov.* Sunny liked that. "Which of the brothers are you?"

"The one who took a double-dog-dare and a black T-shirt. So," Jake asked, "how do you want to work this?"

Five minutes of negotiations and they set the ground rules: arrive in separate cars, pay their own way, and as soon as they'd spent the evening with the Tenacious Trio and danced, that was it, *fini*, end of story.

****

Friday night, Sunny met Debbie, Jan, Troy, and their two husbands and wife—Beck, Sam, and Dee—in the parking lot of Boot Scootin' Bliss and Roadside Grill at straight-up seven o'clock.

"Jake's already here," Troy said with a nod toward the only non-truck in view. He held open the front door to BSBARG, waving the rest of the group inside.

Trying to decide what driving an old, but beautifully maintained, 280-ZX said about a guy, Sunny stumbled down an unmarked step into BSBARG. A medium-height blond man with a Sundance Kid moustache and outlaw smile grabbed her by the waist so she wouldn't fall into him. *My goodness, he had... presence.* If she hadn't already agreed to meet Jake Shane—

"Sunny," Troy said as the man released her, "this is Jake. Jake, Sunny."

Son of a gun.

Jake motioned toward Sunny's blouse. "Where's your T-shirt?"

"In the sack to take to Goodwill. Where's yours?"

"Had to use it to wipe up a drink spill in the car."

Hmm…Now what? Sunny waited while Jake looked around the room. That seemed to be the end of the conversation for now.

Debbie led the group in a non-kicking conga line to a table under a neon *Dos Eques* sign. Sunny noticed mischief in Jake Shane's blue eyes when he seated her and dry humor in his limited contributions to table conversation. She didn't notice the pager clipped to his waistband until he suddenly looked down and rammed his elbow into the basket of onion rings the two of them were sharing. He frowned at the little screen, turned it off, then scooted his chair back and pulled his keys from his front pocket all at the same time.

He gave her a quick nod. "Nice to meet you, Sunny."

Troy shouted, "This doesn't count!"

Jake held up his hand signaling "later" and disappeared into the crowd.

"Isn't he gorgeous?" Jan whispered in Sunny's ear.

Gorgeous? No. Attractive, yes. Very attractive. Gorgeous wouldn't have left me with the tab for his hamburger, beer, and half the onion rings.

****

"Sorry I had to leave like that the other night," Jake said when he called Saturday afternoon.

Sunny balanced the phone on her shoulder while she watered the last of her twenty-five houseplants. "What are you? A doctor?"

"Undercover cop. Listen, Sunny, I'm getting flack from Troy. Will you help me out here? Meet again Friday night and this time we'll dance and I'll win?"

If Troy was hassling Jake, The Tenacious Trio would undoubtedly point out the same rule violation to Sunny at work Monday. Plus, the expectation of meeting an attractive guy again wasn't disheartening. "I'll meet you Friday at seven."

"Thanks! I owe you."

"Yes, you do." Sunny told him what his tab had been.

"Man," he said, "that's outrageous for a beer. I'm

wearing that drink discount T-shirt Friday."

"Not if you want to dance with me."

It would be interesting to see what Jake Shane valued more—winning a dare or a reasonably priced beer.

****

Another Friday, another meeting at Boot Scootin' Bliss and Roadside Grill. Sunny and her friends snaked their way through the happy hour crowd to join Jake at the same table as last week. The BSBARG T-shirt shadowed through his long-sleeved white shirt. *Resourceful.* She liked that.

He leaned back in his chair, an attractive man at ease in his world. "So, what do you do at the newspaper, Sunny?"

She braced for the nodding but blank look of someone numbed by a slideshow. "Graphic design."

"Yeah? Did you see that William Morris exhibit at the college? They insist he was basically a graphic designer."

Odd. Jake looked more fly fisher than gallery gazer. Sunny's brow wrinkled. "What were you doing in the arts building?"

"Cutting through to the jazz concert at the auditorium. Kid brother plays trumpet."

Debbie raised her eyebrows at Sunny. She didn't have to say, "See?" Sunny could do the deducing all by herself. Jake had been in the audience with them that night.

Sunny twirled an onion ring in ketchup. "You like jazz?"

"More of a blues guy."

Again with Debbie's eyebrows. *Puhleez.* "Lots of people besides me like blues," she mouthed at Debbie. When had Debbie turned into such an unabashed matchmake—

Sunny's thought, and most of the noise in BSBARG, disappeared when a heavy velvet darkness dropped over the room. The band wound down to an off-key finish.

Narrowing her eyes, Sunny sought light. She couldn't even see the battery-operated emergency exit signs that had to be somewhere. They were required, right? The sound of chair legs grating against the rough wood floor seemed magnified by the dark, as did the thuds and a sudden ripple of cymbals from the band stage. Little squares of cell phone light appeared like fireflies gathered on the dance floor and around the tables. Cigarette lighters joined to pierce the void with welcome bits of light.

"I hope it's not an electrical short that'll send this place up like a hay bale," Beck said.

Sunny rolled her eyes. *Once a code compliance officer, always a code compliance officer.*

Jake's voice came from beside Sunny. "I'm finishing this beer before I go anywhere." Keys rattled. Jake held up a little flashlight with an intense beam.

The overhead lights came back on in blinding brilliance. A wave of relieved laughter and loud talking followed in its wake. Then off went the lights again. The cell phones and lighters rallied.

Jake propped his flashlight against the catsup bottle. It did nothing for the ambiance, but it did help Sunny spot the food.

"There sure are a lot of cigarette lighters in here for a non-smoking place," he observed.

He'd mentioned he was a cop. Was it a crime to carry a cigarette lighter in a non-smoking establishment? "What do you do undercover?" Sunny asked.

Conversation at their table stopped as quickly as it had when the lights had gone out. Jake leaned toward her, a wide-eyed owl by flashlight. "I beg your pardon?"

"Do you wear disguises or do you just pull on one of those stocking masks?"

Jake tucked his chin.

Sunny shrugged. "You said you were an undercover cop."

"A cop!" Beck blurted just before he launched into a fit of colossal laughter.

"The cops!" came from all over the place. Cigarette lighters clicked off. Amid thumps and a crash on the stage where the band had been playing came a desperate shout.

"Folks, no one's called the cops! It's an electrical problem! That's all!"

The lights flickered, went off, came back on. The crowd had thinned, the band had left, and Jake scowled at

Sunny.

"I was joking about being a cop." He picked up his beer, tipped it back, got nothing so he shook it as if that would produce brew. "I work for the electric company."

"What about the pager?"

"My turn to be on call last week." He put down the bottle. Motioned to the empty stage. "The band's gone," he said as if it was her fault. "Now we can't dance."

"I'll hum a few bars," Sunny said.

"Nope," Troy declared. "Doesn't count."

****

Sunny had never planned to become a regular at the Boot Scootin' Bliss and Roadside Grill, but by the third week folks recognized her and called her by name. She joined the group, *sans* Jake, at their regular table.

She ordered iced tea and then asked, "Where's Jake?"

Troy shrugged and looked at Sam who passed the shrug to Beck. When it had gone around the table and reached Sunny, she said, "He's usually here by now."

"He's usually early," Troy remarked.

"Maybe he had to stop for gas," Sam said.

"Maybe he's caught in traffic," Jan added.

Sunny knew one thing for certain; when Jake did turn up they would dance first. No chance of him getting paged away. No chance of the band disappearing. Dance and win the dare.

"Sunny?" Troy leaned toward her after Debbie, Jan, and Dee gave the waitress their order. "Are you gonna have anything?"

Sunny flashed the server a smile. "I'm not hungry just yet, thanks."

Jake still hadn't arrived by the time Sunny was nibbling on Debbie's soggy, cold French fries. Tapping her foot in rhythm to the music, she said, "I wonder if I should call Jake. You know, be sure he's all right."

Everyone looked at her. She could hear the unspoken message. Jake was a big guy. He could take care of himself.

The new band was excellent and more people boot-scooted on the dance floor than had the past two weeks. One good dance song followed the other. Sunny talked and laughed and kept glancing at the clock. The least the guy could do was call.

"Maybe he had car trouble," she said after Jan and Sam strolled to the dance floor. After all, that was an old ZX.

"Maybe," Debbie said, "he's left you a message."

Her cell phone! Why hadn't Sunny thought of that? *Well, good heavens*. When had she turned it off? The moment the little screen lit she saw she had missed three calls. She went to the relative quiet of the restroom to listen to them.

"Sunny, it's Jake. I'll be late. Wrapping up a job here." He sounded hassled.

"Sunny, it's Jake again. Man, I'm sorry about this. I think the band plays until one. Hang in there." He sounded worried.

"Sunny, it's Jake. Well shoot... I'll call you right back." He sounded tired.

Given that the last call had been more than an hour ago, Jake and she were obviously not going to meet each other or the dare this week. Despite protests, Sunny called it an evening and walked to the parking lot. She'd no more started her car than her cell phone rang.

"Why don't you ever answer your phone?" Jake greeted her. Instead of waiting for an answer—as if Sunny owed him one anyhow—he asked, "Where are you?"

How could she possibly be relieved and angry at the same time? "The west parking lot. Where are you?"

"Just got into the east parking lot. Did you save me a dance?"

"Aren't you too tired?"

"For the cotton-eyed Joe, yeah. For a really slow dance, no. We'll just do this and get it over with."

Do it and get it over with! Sunny had waited for hours, even been sort of worried, only for him to talk about her like some annoying chore?

"You know what, Jake. I don't have time right now. Let's try for next week." She turned off her cell phone and was gone like that stupid BSBARG T-shirt she planned to throw in the garbage as soon as she got home.

****

A double-dog-dare. She had given up three Friday

nights because Troy had double-dog-dared her to go dancing with his buddy, Jake Shane, at Boot Scootin' Bliss and Roadside Grill.

How sad was that?

The best way Sunny had found to get over the disappointment without getting fat was to get busy. Saturday morning she had the oil changed in the car, called all the family to catch up, finished the Hillerman book, and wrapped her gift for Maggie's tenth birthday party and cook-out late that afternoon. It seemed like just yesterday Sunny had stood at the hospital nursery window admiring Dee and Troy's little girl. The fact the years had passed so quickly concerned Sunny. It also kept her from concentrating on the matter at hand, which was the new side gate to Dee and Troy's backyard propelling her backwards.

"See?" Jake had his eyes on Troy completely unaware of Sunny's staggering. "This needs to swing in toward the yard so—"

Troy stepped around Jake and grabbed Sunny's right elbow, saving her from falling into the flowerbed. Jake leaned back against the gate to hold it open and offered a waning smile.

First Jake stood her up at BSBARG. Now he nearly bashed her into the yellow rose bush. And he had the nerve to smile? Sunny retrieved the gift, thanked Troy, and stomped past Jake into the backyard.

Over by the swimming pool, a dozen kids shouted, laughed, dunked, and splashed. The adults scattered around in cordial groups sipping drinks while enjoying friendly conversation. Smoke from the grill drifted across Sunny's face. When it cleared, a frowning Jake blocked her way.

"I left three messages on your cell phone last night, and you act like you're mad."

"I assure you, Jake, it is no act." Sunny raised her chin. "Now if you'll excuse—"

"Uncle Jake?" Maggie shouted from the pool deck. "Can you throw us in the pool now? Hi, Sunny!"

Uncle? Was Jake Dee's brother?

"No," Dee said when Sunny and she stood alone in

the kitchen, "Jake's not related. He might as well be, though. Troy and he have been friends since kindergarten."

Leaning toward the window, Sunny watched a boy grasp Jake's hands, walk up his legs, and then somersault. With a huge grin, Jake sat on his heels so the boy and he could exchange high-fives.

"Why haven't I seen Jake around before?" She turned at a nudge from Dee, and took the stack of plastic plates bound for the picnic table.

"No idea," Dee said. "He was only away in Austin for a couple of years."

Jake gave Sunny sideways looks during the hamburger dinner, the blowing out of candles, the slicing of cake, and the opening of presents. He kept his distance until he followed a few steps behind when she walked toward her car.

"Sunny?"

Jake stepped in front of her. He shifted from one boot to the other. Hands stuck in his pockets, he rattled his keys and looked everywhere but at her.

"What?" she asked when she couldn't take the suspense any longer.

Jake licked his lips and rubbed the back of his neck.

Oh for crying out loud. Sunny stepped off the curb. Jake cleared his throat and mumbled. Sunny was darned if she would ask again. She took a deep breath and put on the most patient face possible.

Jake leaned close and whispered, "I can't dance."

****

His admission might have been a ruse so Sunny would allow him in her house that evening except for one thing—no one could fake those moves. He had a great sense of rhythm, evidenced by the way he tapped his foot and snapped his fingers. He just couldn't dance. Given his lack of finesse, a slow dance seemed best. Or maybe not. Slow dancing meant holding hands. Involved his palm resting at the back of her shoulder blades. Necessitated her left elbow riding just above his right. She'd never been so distracted by a dancing partner in all her life.

"Maybe we should take a break," Jake suggested when she checked the air conditioner thermostat for the fifth time in an hour.

A glass of iced tea on the front porch sounded good.

Jake had grown up in Fort Worth, he told her while they watched lightning bugs. His mother taught high school. His father was a policeman.

"A cop for real," he hastened to add. "A few years ago I was in love, but it turned out she wasn't. I have two dogs, Cut and Shoot. I like to cook, hate to mop, and don't like winter." He tilted his glass at Sunny. "Your turn."

"I'm from here. Have an older sister who's married and has two kids." Best not to share how single she felt at gatherings now. No fault of the family's. "Mom runs an art gallery. Dad has an insurance agency. You've met my cat. I love to cook, and my next house will be an earth shelter."

He grinned. "You skipped the romance part."

"Train wrecks, except for Steve."

Jake's eyes narrowed. "Sorry to hear that."

"Steve was great. When he wasn't promoted to eighth grade, it broke my heart. But counseling helped."

Did she just imagine that he looked relieved?

"So," he said after a long sigh, "do you think if we worked on this a couple more nights I could pass as a dancer?"

Hmm. She liked that idea.

****

Newspaper ad design didn't seem nearly as important as watching the workday countdown on her desk clock the next three days. No overtime for Sunny now. No talking in the parking lot. She was outta there. Zipping to a restaurant to get take-out when it was her turn to provide dinner, hurrying home to swap her professional clothes for jeans and a T-shirt when it wasn't, hoping she looked calm and collected by the time Jake showed up on the front porch.

By Wednesday, he had slow dancing down, and they agreed to meet at BSBARG after work on Thursday for a test dance. Time warped that day at work. Every second seemed an hour; every hour a day. Keyboards tick-clacked and phones summoned. Troy put a Trace Atkins CD in the player, and drink cans chimed in with their empty predecessors in the recycle bin. Everyone else behaved as if life was normal. But it wasn't. After Sunny mistakenly emailed the ad designs for a bank to a car dealer, the day stretched like well-chewed gum.

****

Sunny drove straight to BSBARG at 5:30, despite her admittedly foul mood. Jake ran up the walk to open the door for her. "You okay?"

"It was a rotten day."

"No kidding. Long as a sermon, too."

They staked their claim at the usual table. He picked up the cracked-plastic menu. "What sounds good?"

"Not a burger and onion rings."

"Pizza?" He peeked over the menu and she nodded. "What do you want on it?"

"Surprise me."

Jake slapped down the menu. "I've made decisions all day, Sunny. I don't want to decide about pizza toppings."

"I never figured you for a whiner."

"I never figured you to pass the buck."

They asked Macy, their server-for-tonight, to surprise them. The artichoke and grilled chicken pizza was good. Very good.

"That was kind of a small pizza." Jake leaned back, slowly rotating his beer bottle on the paper coaster. "Wanna get another one?" he asked, then took a slug of beer.

"Sure. We can take home what's left and have it for breakfast."

High velocity beer pelted Sunny's shirt, the table, the empty pizza dish, and the stragglers dripped down Jake's chin. Sunny was pretty sure he wasn't choking. She'd always heard if the lips aren't blue and the person's coughing loudly, don't interfere and for sure don't slap their back.

She flagged Macy and ordered a clone pizza, then excused herself and went to the ladies' room. The hand dryer did a decent job on her shirt, but she smelled like a walking keg party when she returned to the table. Jake sat slumped, straw-sipping water from a plastic tumbler.

"Beer go down your windpipe?" Sunny asked.

She recognized the owlish look from the night she'd asked him about his undercover work. He leaned forward and said, "I don't think you heard what you said."

Of course she had. "Beer go down your windpipe."

Jake folded his arms on the tabletop, dipping his right elbow in a beer pond. "We can take home what's left and have it for breakfast."

Sunny pointed to his beer bottle. "It's empty, and who on earth drinks flat beer for breakfast?"

He slid his right hand from his nose to his chin, then back up to his forehead, which he slowly rubbed. "The way you said we can take some home...and have it for breakfast...sounded like you were inviting me to spend the night."

"You think I'm that kind of woman?"

"I know you're not." Jake stood, held out his left hand. "Tell you what, while we're waiting for that pizza, let's dance."

Dancing for pizza took four songs from the CD jukebox. Sunny had the first dance with Jake, but everyone was into being social, swapping partners, and getting acquainted. Jake stood out the second and third dances, talking to women and rubbing his left knee as if he'd hurt it. The fourth dance was a slow dance. With Jake. And he must have been practicing on his own time, because he finally took the lead.

Sunny could learn a lot about a man by dancing with him. Did he lead like a Neanderthal hauling her to his cave, or did he pilot so effortlessly that she didn't even notice? Did he hold her hand as if she were a professional arm wrestler, or was his touch gentle? Did he balk when she saw an impending collision behind him and urged him one way or the other, or did he quickly adapt and thank her for the save? Did he get huffy at a misstep, or did he shrug and smile, or better yet pretend he didn't notice?

Jake danced just the way Sunny liked.

Back at their table, they shared pizza and sipped their iced tea. Jake was a one-beer guy. Sunny liked that. He also tipped big. She liked that, too.

Sunny didn't notice BSBARG had filled up until the jukebox yielded to the band. Another practice session on the dance floor—a couple dance, then a line dance that Jake gamely tried, then a triple two-step with a guy named Dan who actually had to be told to take off his spurs. Jake stood outside the rail around the dance floor, watching and smiling. When Sunny and Jake slow danced together again he said, "You're a good dancer."

"I'd rather just dance with you."

He smiled. "Me, too. But this is a friendly place, and as long as a guy asks me if it's okay to dance with you then—"

What!

Sunny stalked off the dance floor and Jake followed. He asked, "Are you all right?" all the way to the table.

"No, I am not all right." Sunny sat because standing blocked the access to the dance floor. "I am not a possession that you give permission to other men to use."

"For crying out loud, Sunny! It's just good etiquette." Jake motioned toward the dance floor. "I wouldn't walk up and ask one of those attached women to dance. It'd put her in a bad spot because she'd have to chose between him and me."

"You don't think I can decide who I want to dance with?"

Jake plopped into his chair. "I think you're capable of doing anything you darn well want to."

"And I'm supposed to be flattered that you think that?"

"If I wanted to sweet-talk you, Sunny, I know a hundred other ways to do it."

"Oh really?"

His chin jutted and his eyes narrowed. "Really."

"Maybe I don't sweet-talk."

"I'm pretty sure you don't." Jake's deep chuckle tickled all the way to Sunny's toes.

And so, she was left to wonder—sweet talk immunity, good or bad?

****

Friday night. Back at BSBARG sharing a table with Jake, waiting on The Tenacious Trio and Spouses. Jake's remark that he knew a hundred ways to sweet talk Sunny if he wanted to still rankled. Almost as much as the thought that he considered her sweet talk proof, which led her to the dreadful discovery that just maybe she didn't want to be sweet talk proof.

Troy sent a text message to Jake at 7:30. The

babysitter hadn't shown up at Debbie and Beck's yet.

"Sounds like we're in for a wait." When Sunny didn't reply, Jake rolled his eyes. "Tell me what I did wrong, and I'll apologize."

"I shouldn't have to tell you."

"We've had this conversation before, Sunny."

All right then. "I am not a possession that you give permission to other men to use."

Jake crossed his arms on the table. "We've had that conversation before, too."

Darn him anyhow.

The band started a song Sunny knew well. Lyrics about dancing, sudden discovery, overwhelming feelings, kissing, and spinning around.

Jake stood, held out his hand. "Maybe we just need to dance."

Their first kiss was the lead singer's fault, and the songwriter the accomplice. The second kiss was faultless. The third kiss made conversation unnecessary.

Debbie, Beck, Jan, Sam, Dee, and Troy arrived at the table about nine. Sunny and Jake waited while their friends ate their burgers and fries. When anyone suggested they dance, Jake said the floor was too crowded or he didn't like the song, and then he brought up subjects sure to stimulate lots of talk and laughter. Ten minutes before closing, he stood and scooted Sunny out of her chair.

They danced near the center of the floor. Sunny scarcely moved her feet. She kept her elbows in tight, snugged to Jake so she wouldn't bump anyone else. Mercy, she could use something cold to drink.

Jake gave her the smile of a winner who is still learning to be gracious. "We've won the double-dog-dare," he said. "We came in separate cars. We paid our own way. We spent the evening with our friends, and we danced."

Sunny's breath snagged in her throat. Would Jake hold her to the rest of their agreement? Say this was it, *fini*, end of story? Could she have misread him that badly?

His lips near her right ear, Jake whispered, "I want to renegotiate that very last part of our agreement."

Sunny liked that.

A lot.

About the Author

I have lately realized printer's ink is in my blood. My first job was with a newspaper, and after almost as many careers as Mark Twain had, my last job was with a magazine. I am fortunate to be able to write about what I know and love—the people and history of my native state of Texas. Thanks to NTRWA and The Wild Rose Press for letting me share this story with you.

The Ring

by

Christine Crocker

*Love at first sight,
it happens!*

Christie Crocker

Dedication

This story is dedicated to my own Texan hero, my wonderful husband and inspiration, David. Thank you, Darling, for believing in me, as well as giving me your wholehearted support and encouragement in all that I do. I love you.

Jeannie stopped pacing long enough to glance at her watch. *Charlie should be home anytime now.* Her stomach churned with nerves. She pulled the drapes back from the living room window and stared outside. It was a beautiful blue-sky Texas day and typically deceptive from inside the cool air-conditioned confines of the house. Except for the occasional ripple of an errant breeze through the drooping leaves on the crepe myrtle, the air outside was still and oppressive she knew.

Every year the relentless summer heat caused the tall graceful tree to weep sap on any vehicle parked beneath it. Every summer Charlie threatened to cut it down. This summer was no different. Besides the sticky dew that filmed the windshield, he hated the way the magenta blooms stuck to the body of his pride and joy, his pickup truck. Still she refused to let him cut down the tree.

She'd been ignorant about crepe myrtles when she'd first planted the tree so long ago. All the crepe myrtles she'd ever seen had been small bushes. How could she have known the city fathers had decided to beautify the town and call it the 'Crepe Myrtle Capital of Texas'? All the crepe myrtles she'd seen were newly planted, hence their small size. How could she have known the lovely little bush would grow into the towering tree that now arched gracefully over the driveway? She shook her head and heaved a heartfelt sigh. *How many times had they had the same argument?*

"I hate the way that stupid tree pees all over my truck," he'd grouse. "We should cut it down."

"Park closer to the house if it bothers you so much," she'd say. "Or next to the fence." It should have been an easy solution to a simple problem but Charlie was just as stubborn about his parking place as she was about keeping the tree. Stalemate.

It wasn't the only point of contention, but it seemed to typify their disagreements. Nothing big overall, but an accumulation of little things which had built up over the years. This latest disagreement was threatening to explode into something bigger than she was certain she could handle with diplomacy, let alone grace.

Jeannie's hand was clenched in a tight fist. She opened her hand until her fingers curled loosely above the ring she held. Deep indentations creased her palm from clasping it so tightly. A simple band of yellow and white gold, it had left her finger only once in twenty-five years of marriage. Twenty-five years of joys and sorrows bound in a circle of metal that symbolized love, friendship and eternal devotion. It gleamed with dull warmth, its once sharp edges worn to a rounded luster. The emblem of my married life, she thought with a pang. *How can I part with it?* Without the ring on her finger she felt naked and exposed. The white flesh where she'd worn the ring was stark against her tanned hand.

A tear rolled down her cheek and plopped onto her palm. She recalled the day Charlie had placed the ring upon her finger. He'd been so worried about losing the ring he had jammed it onto his little finger. The frantic look on his face when he couldn't get it off at the right time had caused her to burst into laughter. The Justice of the Peace who'd married them said a marriage that began with laughter was bound to last. Another tear fell and was followed by more. The ring became an island in a pool of tears.

Laughter. They'd certainly had a lot of it during their marriage. She smiled at the memory of her first sight of Charlie. Theirs had been a whirlwind romance. So young, they'd only thought they knew what love was.

A recent transplant to Texas, she'd gone to her first rodeo with friends from work. The Cowbell, they told her, was a small venue. The first indoor rodeo in Texas, it was a place where aspiring cowboys could hone their skills.

The bull-riding event had already begun by the time Jeannie and her friends bought their tickets and found seats. She'd been adjusting to the acrid smell of horses and cattle and their offending by-products mixed with the smell of popcorn and hotdogs which wafted through the surprisingly cool air when shouts and groans drew her attention to the arena. The announcer's laughter was a tinny echo in the high-ceilinged building as he razzed the hapless rider who'd just been tossed like a rag doll from his perch atop a two-thousand-pound whirlwind of a bull.

Her heart went out to the lanky cowboy who pulled himself out of the dirt while the clowns distracted the bull. He limped over to the center of the ring and bent to pick his black cowboy hat up out of the dust. As he straightened, his gaze locked with hers. Her breath stopped in her lungs. Time froze. At the same instant he rocked back on his heels as if physically pushed. Then a slow wide smile curved his lips and a dimple popped into his left cheek. He slapped the hat against his thigh to dislodge the dirt and dust and plopped it back on his curly auburn hair. All the while his good-humored stare never left hers.

A giddy thrill shot through her. *Oh my God.* Goose bumps prickled the flesh on her arms. *This is the one.* Mesmerized, she watched him saunter to the end of the ring where he was handed his bull-riding rig with what seemed to be an inordinate amount of ribbing from the cowboys who opened the gate for him. He turned and tipped his hat to her before disappearing into the mysterious depths where the animals were stabled. When he didn't reappear, she felt a stab of disappointment. *Am I just being fanciful?* she thought. No. The connection had definitely been electric. The energy in their shared glance had positively zinged between them. It was fate. Love at first sight. Now she knew why the French called it a *coup de foudre,* a stroke of lightning, as her body tingled from the shock of that instant recognition. They'd meet again. She just knew it.

She took a deep, cleansing breath to control the jumping nerves in her stomach. Although her mind was no longer interested in the rodeo, she forced her attention back to the action in the ring. Several more riders met the dirt in quick succession. So far, the tally was bulls seven, humans zero.

The couple she'd come with went to get soft drinks at the concession stand and left her to guard their seats. She gazed idly at the people around her. Teenage girls and women she thought old enough to know better wore jeans so tight you could tell if a quarter was heads or tails in the back pocket. Figure-hugging Rocky Mountain jeans were paired with colorful western shirts and matching cowboy hats and boots. Belts cinched tight around impossibly tiny waists sported saucer-sized silver buckles. Many of the hats trailed colorful feathers from the hatbands. Who'd have thought you could buy pink cowboy hats? And purple cowboy boots? The mind boggled.

A booted foot stepped over the seat next to her, and as she turned to protest the intrusion her nose caught the clean smell of soap and citrus scented aftershave.

"Mind if I sit here?" a low baritone drawled politely.

"I'm sorry, my friends...." Her voice trailed off. *My cowboy.* The man slipped his lithe frame into the space next to her. He'd changed his shirt, and, judging from the damp, slicked-back waves of hair, had taken time for a quick cleanup. Her heart tumbled in her chest and skipped a beat. Two, three beats. "Oh, sh-sure," she stuttered. All coherent thought left her brain. He smiled, and she felt her face flush. For the life of her she couldn't think of a thing to say and stared dumbly into his face. *Am I a dingbat or what?* She cast around her mind for something intelligent to say. Thankfully he took up the conversational gambit before she could trip over her own tongue.

"Charles Cochran." He stuck out his broad hand. "But you can call me Charlie."

She touched her shaking fingers to his. "Jean Landers," she said shyly. "But you can call me Jeannie." Her hand was engulfed in his warm grasp.

"Jeannie. I like it. I haven't seen you here before." The dimple in his cheek flashed and she wondered what it would be like to press her lips to his cheek and dip the tip of her tongue into that enticing indentation.

"Umm—no." She shook her head to focus on not making a fool of herself. "It's my first rodeo." She smiled back at him and quickly bit her lip, conscious as ever of her crooked eyetooth.

He flashed her a smile full of sunshine and warmth. "You're not from around here, are you?"

"What gave me away?" She couldn't help but return

his infectious smile.

"Well, here abouts, we don't say ro-day-oh. It's ro-dee-oh. But I reckon we can forgive you since you're a Yankee and don't know no better," he said with an exaggerated Texas accent.

"Ah hah! I'll have you know I was born in Mississippi. So you can take back the bit about being a Yankee," she said smugly.

"You sure about that? I don't hear any "Magnolia State" in your voice." His right eyebrow quirked upward and his lips pursed as he studied her. "Nope. I'd say this is the first time you've even been south of the Red River."

She laughed. "I guess you've got me there. The truth is my father was stationed at Keesler Air Force Base in Biloxi and I was only there long enough to be born before we moved to California."

"Ooh!" He winced. "That's worse. A prune picker."

"Prune picker? I'm no such thing." She punched him lightly on the arm.

He caught her hand in his and wrapped his fingers comfortably around hers. "Better watch what you're doing, Ma'am." He tipped his hat with his free hand. "I might have to take you into custody for assaulting an officer of the law."

"You're a lawman?"

"Yes, Ma'am. Don't let my goat-roper getup fool you. I'm a duly sworn sheriff's deputy." His solemn expression was spoiled by the twinkle in his eyes.

"And what is a duly sworn deputy doing getting tossed off bulls at the Friday night ro-dee-oh?"

"It's just something I do for fun." He shrugged.

"Getting thrown off a bull is your idea of fun? Seems you could find something a little less painful to do with your time."

He chuckled. "Shoot. It's not that bad. *The Cowbell* doesn't have any really bad bulls. Most of the riders are high school kids and wannabes."

"Wannabes?"

"Guys who can't follow the circuit either for lack of talent or money, or both." He grinned.

"Since you're clearly not a high school kid does that make you a wannabe?" She teased.

He laughed out loud. His boisterous guffaw had several of the tight jeans crowd glancing their way. "No. I did a little bull-riding in high school but decided, wisely I might add, it wasn't the career for me. The only reason I'm here tonight is a reunion of sorts. A bunch of guys from my high school rodeo team decided to sign-up for a bit of 'remember when'."

"And has it lived up to your fond memories?"

"To tell you the truth, I don't remember the ride being so short or the dirt being so hard." He rubbed his leg. "I imagine I'm really going to feel sore tomorrow. My buddy Kyle is next up." He went on to explain the intricacies of bull-riding to her as Kyle prepared to ride. "The total score a rider can get is 100 points. Fifty points are based how hard the bull is to ride. The other fifty points goes to how well the rider performs. The judge looks for good control and body position and gives extra style points if the rider can rake the bull's shoulders with his spurs."

"Spurs? Doesn't that hurt them?" She glanced at his tooled leather cowboy boots. He wasn't wearing any spurs.

He shook his head. "The spurs are blunt. If a rider uses spurs that cut a bull they're immediately disqualified."

"Then why wear them?"

"For extra style points and also to serve as an irritant if the bull isn't performing well." He shrugged. "Some guys even claim it helps them stay atop their ride. The hardest part though is staying on for a full eight seconds holding on with only one hand." He stood up suddenly pulling her up with him. "Yeehaw, Kyle!" He whooped as the buzzer sounded and Kyle completed a full eight-second ride.

She giggled at his exuberance for his friend. "And how long did you stay on? Two seconds? I think you made a wise decision to stick to law enforcement." She nudged him with her elbow.

He heaved an exaggerated sigh and pressed his hand to heart, flinching dramatically. "You've wounded me. A man just can't get no respect." He tucked her arm up under his and pulled her closer. "You've impugned my integrity, Ma'am. I gave you fair warning. Consider yourself in custody."

He'd taken her into custody, all right. Two weeks later they stood before the Justice of the Peace in Waxahachie and pledged their lives to each other. They'd been young, impetuous, and in love. Friends told her it would never last. She was making a mistake. Nobody gets married without getting to know each other first. She'd live to regret her hasty marriage.

How wrong they all were. She turned the worn gold band over in her hand. She had only one regret. Another tear splashed against her hand. *How could she tell Charlie she'd changed her mind? He'd be so hurt.* Her fingers curled tight over the ring again. *How could she make him understand? Would he?*

The kitchen door slammed shut. Charlie was home.

"Jeannie?" he called.

"In here, Honey." She called him into the living room. She turned to him as he entered the room, a bouquet of yellow roses clutched in one hand. His trademark dimple punctuated his beaming smile.

"Happy anniversary, Darling."

Her gaze drank in his dear face. His once-deep auburn curls were liberally mixed with white and his warm brown eyes radiated love and devotion. His lanky frame had filled out over the years into a comfortable cushion matching her own generous curves. *God, she loved this man. And now she was going to hurt him.*

He set the flowers on the end table, wrapped her in a bear hug and kissed her. Despite the passion of their embrace, she knew when he sensed her disquiet. He held her at arms length and studied her face. "You've been crying." A worried frown furrowed his brow. "What's wrong?"

She bit her lip and searched for words to explain how she felt. The wedding band burned in her fist. Nothing to do but take the plunge. "Honey," she began. Her voice wobbled as she struggled for the right words. Words to take the sting out of her rejection. "You know how much I love you. From the first moment I saw you pulling yourself out of the dust of that rodeo arena I knew I was going to marry you."

Charlie nodded and smiled, the dimple she loved so

much popping into place. "I love you too, Honey."

She held up her hand and revealed the wedding band. "I can't do it." Tears spurted and she swiped them away. "You always promised you were going to buy me a fancy diamond ring set." She couldn't look at his face. Why was this so hard? She felt like she was throwing everything away. But she wasn't. She had to make him understand. His arms tightened around her but she pulled away from him and broke free. She walked over to the coffee table, picked up a small square box and held it out to her husband. He took it from her.

Suddenly the words came in a torrent. Her heart eased. "I love my wedding band. I can't stop wearing it. You placed it on my hand twenty-five years ago and it's as much a part of me as breathing. All my memories of our life are bound in this symbol of our love. I can't discard it for something new and shiny. It's my comfort, just like you are." She burst into gulping sobs.

"Aw, Honey." Charlie engulfed her in the shelter of his arms. She breathed in the deep, comforting scent of him. The slight citrus tang of his aftershave mingled with the starch of his wilted uniform. He lifted her chin up to his. "Hey, you're gonna make me cry if you don't stop." He wiped the tears from her eyes with his thumbs. "I'm supposed to be the sentimental one around here."

She hiccupped and gave a watery laugh. "I know. Who woulda thunk it, hunh?"

"Yeah." He pulled her to his chest and rested his chin atop her head. "I always felt bad about not being able to give you a diamond engagement ring. Bad enough I rushed you to a Justice of the Peace and cheated you out of a fancy wedding." He sighed. "I thought the new ring set would make you happy."

"I've always been happy. I was in just as much hurry as you to marry. You didn't cheat me out of anything. It doesn't take a diamond ring to make me happy. You make me happy, Honey." She lifted her face up for his kiss. He pulled her down onto the couch.

"But I upset you." He looked disappointed. "I thought you wanted it."

"I thought I did too, but when push came to shove I couldn't do it. The diamond wedding ring set is beautiful but I can't replace my wedding band." She shifted to a more comfortable position and showed him the ring. "This ring has meaning. Remember the time I lost it in the swimming pool out at the farm?"

"Do I ever? Dad tried to get you to get out of the pool. He said he'd buy you another one." He shook his head recalling her stubbornness.

"And I said it was my wedding band and another one just wouldn't be the same. It got dark and the temperature dropped and you came and ordered me to get out of the pool because you were afraid I'd get sick. I insisted on one last dive. I dove in and as my finger scraped the bottom of the pool the ring slid right onto it. I was so relieved and overjoyed to have found my ring. And it only took four hours of searching every inch of that pool."

"You were also a wrinkled prune. And you did get sick." He gave her a tight squeeze. "My little prune-picker."

"Hey!" She punched him in the arm. "Who're you calling a prune-picker?"

He winced and rubbed his arm. "You shouldn't have done that you know. I may have to charge you with assault and battery."

"And take me into custody?" She looped her arms around his neck and nuzzled his cheek. "Is that a promise, Sheriff?"

"Consider yourself under arrest." His eyes took on a wolfish gleam. "But first things first." He took the ring from her and pressed her left hand to his lips. His warm gaze held hers as he slipped the wedding band back to its rightful place on her finger. He wrapped his arms around her and leaned back into the cushions, breaking off their kiss to come up for air.

"All better now?" he asked, kissing away the last traces of tears from her eyes.

She nodded. "All better."

He squeezed her tightly. "Good."

They snuggled in comfortable silence, Jeannie marveling once again how lucky she was to have Charlie. All was right with their world.

"By the way," Charlie murmured, his breath tickling

her ear.

"Hmmm?" She gave a contented sigh and smiled. "About that damn crepe myrtle..."

About the Author

Christine Crocker is a naturalized Texan, having lived in the town of Joshua, Texas for 33 of her 35 years of marriage. She has worked as a chili pepper picker, a nurse aide, an opera singer, and is currently a church music director as well as a writer. Like her heroine in *The Ring*, she married her husband David soon after meeting him.

The Rancher's Wife

by

Jen FitzGerald

Dedication

To God Most High for His Glory

Chapter One

Molly Miller's eyes snapped open.

The last time she'd checked, her bed did not sit under a huge oak tree. Nor was her mattress this hard and layered with dirt and leaves.

Molly sat up, easing the kinks out of her lower back. Her shirtwaist was wrinkled and a large smudge of dirt adorned the right side of her skirt. The faint scent of burnt hide, cow manure, and smoke carried on the hot breeze. It ruffled the errant strands of hair that escaped her long plait. She picked up the end tied with dark blue ribbon. When has she dyed her hair this lovely shade of mahogany?

Wait... Shirtwaist, skirt, plait? She hadn't worn her hair in a braid since grade school. Where on God's green earth was she?

And since when did she use that expression?

"Molly! Molly May Miller, where the heck are ya, girl? It's time to eat."

Molly headed toward the large stone house on the hill. A strange sense of déjà vu rippled through her. She knew this place, and yet she didn't. This must be how Alice felt after falling down the rabbit hole.

"There you are, Daughter. You gotta be the disappearingest girl in the state of Texas."

Texas?

"I'm sorry, Papa." She kissed his grizzled cheek. "I was reading under the tree and I must've dozed off." Molly ascended the porch stairs and entered the house. Rough-hewn beams glowed golden in the late afternoon sunlight pouring in through the huge picture windows. The same large rocks that covered the outside of the house framed the great fireplace. The savory scent of a pot roast filled the air and her stomach grumbled.

But she didn't eat red meat.

Oh, but I do. I live on a cattle ranch...

Molly looked around, but didn't see anyone other than Papa, who followed her into the dining room.

Texas? Cattle ranch? But she'd never been to a ranch or to Texas.

"Hello, Molly. You made a mighty pretty picture out there under that tree." The man's deep voice washed over her.

Who was this handsome stranger and why, all of a sudden, did she feel perturbed and thrilled to her toes at the same time? The thrill she could understand; he was gorgeous. Short, strawberry-blonde hair spiked above his forehead in a charming fashion and dark lashes ringed his gray eyes. Faded denim hugged long, lean legs. Something else about him nagged at her, but it eluded her at the moment.

The long, oak plank table overflowed with bowls and platters of food. Papa took his place at the head of the table, tucking a large red and white checked napkin into his collar. "Zach here, came over to iron out the details of the wedding."

Wedding? Whose wedding?

Her heart raced.

Wait a minute.

Then it hit her—the romance novel she'd been reading before going to bed last night, The Rancher's Wife. Well, she didn't remember going to bed exactly. She'd just wanted a few hours of entertainment. And now, somehow, she was playing the role of the heroine. And if memory served, the wedding wasn't too far off.

Papa forked a huge slice of gravy-laden beef and a mountain of mashed potatoes onto his plate.

The smell of sweat, fresh air and sunshine hit her like a horse hoof to the gut as Zach stepped behind her and pulled out her chair.

Um, okay, wow.

She couldn't remember the last time a guy pulled out a chair for her. Some time during her first semester at the community college back in North Platte, maybe.

Once she was seated, he moved around to take the chair opposite her. And if his delicious male scent and gentlemanly way wasn't enough to render her breathless, the contrast of a starched white shirt against his sun-bronzed skin surely was. His rolled-up sleeves revealed crinkly brown hairs along muscled forearms. The same crisp brown hairs that peeked at her from the vee of his open collar. Was he that color all over?

What in heaven's name are you thinking?

"What?" Molly glanced around looking for the source of the voice, but she was the only woman in the room.

Zach's eyebrows rose in a neat arch. Her tone must've been a little sharper than necessary.

"Zach was jus' askin' how you felt about St. Louis for yer wedding trip," Papa said around a mouthful of string beans. "No need to get yer tail hairs in a tangle."

Unease rushed over her like a gully washer.

What in the world was going on here? Why did she feel so out of sorts?

Oh. Oh, no...

You've got to be kidding. How did she get into these things? She wasn't just playing the heroine in this crazy X-Files episode; evidently she was sharing the role with the rightful owner. She guessed. If a character in a book could be considered the owner of the role.

Where was Special Agent Fox Mulder when she needed him?

"Molly?"

But that voice. And those eyes.

"Um..." Molly pulled her gaze from her apparent betrothed to the food on the table and filled her plate.

"We could ride the river boat. What do you think?" Zach asked.

She took a bite of beef to avoid an immediate answer and almost moaned aloud at the rich, melt-in-your-mouth flavor.

But some sort of sound must have escaped her. Zach's eyes widened and then darkened a shade or two, from early-morning-sky gray to thundercloud-on-the-prairie gray. She knew what that look meant and a spark of awareness settled in her stomach. Papa smacked away at his beef, oblivious to the sudden charge in the room.

Now look what you've gone and done. He's got that look.

Yes, he does. She'd give her eyeteeth to see a look

75

like that directed at her. Just once. Love and desire was a heady combination.

Love? He doesn't love me. He loves this ranch.

Well, that cleared things up a bit. Apparently, her alter ego didn't believe her man loved her.

"We could go all the way to Omaha, if you like," Zach said. The lightness of his tone belied the heaviness of his gaze.

Molly jumped from her seat and threw her napkin to the table. Both men looked at her in astonishment. "I'm not going to St. Louis, and I'm not going to Omaha. The wedding's off."

Chapter Two

Surprise and hurt flashed across Zach's face, but Molly ignored it and hurried from the room, Papa's stuttering outrage following her out the door.

How dare he plan her honeymoon without her? Or her wedding, for that matter.

A wave of dizziness washed over her. She grabbed the handrail as she stumbled down the porch steps. She gasped, taking deep draughts of air until her breathing evened out.

The sun, now below the horizon, left the ranch square in deepening purple shadows. The whirring and chirruping of the katydids fought the low bawling of hungry calves in search of their mothers.

She rushed past the barn and the outbuildings and headed for her secret place. Well, not completely secret. Zach knew.

She crossed the creek bed and crawled up on the huge, round boulder. Its smooth, flat surface still held the heat of the day. She pulled her legs to her chest, wrapping her arms around them, and rested her chin on her knees.

She'd known this day was coming. Anticipated it. But now that it was here, she wasn't really prepared. And her earlier confidence drained away like the heat of the day.

In the time it took for Zach to arrive and settle on the boulder next to her, Molly had watched the moon rise from behind the large hackberry tree. Of course he'd followed her. She hadn't expected him not to.

That singular scent that was Zach wafted over her. Why, oh, why, did the man have to smell so good all the time? It always weakened her resolve around him.

"Remember the day I first found you out here?"

Boy, did she. She was twelve. Papa yelled at her for some infraction and she took off. She fell asleep in a small hollowed out cave next to this dried-up creek bed about a mile from the homestead.

Tired and sweaty when he'd come across her, he gallantly offered to tote her home on his back. That was the first time she smelled a man who wasn't her papa. She'd never forgotten.

"You were so excited about your adventure, you chattered all the way back to the ranch. Near to took my left ear off."

Yes, and when she'd been bathed and fed, Papa gave her a lickin' for running off and causing so much trouble for everybody.

"You can't just not talk to me. It won't solve anything."

She sighed. Couldn't he just let her be mad for a while? And what difference did it make whether they married or not? Papa was grooming him to take over the ranch anyway. Why did she need to be involved? Maybe she could go back East to school or something. That'd be exciting.

Only she didn't want to leave. She loved the ranch, and she loved Zach.

"I want to marry you, Molly."

"I know you do." But not, 'I love you, Molly.'

"I thought you wanted to marry me, too."

"I did." She still did, truth be told. She'd loved him for as long as she could remember. But how could she marry a man she no longer knew? Or one who didn't love her in return.

Zach hung his head. She couldn't mean that. All that kept him going the last two years of working the ranch and dealing with her father was the thought of making her his wife.

That stupid promise...

"Molly...," His mouth dried up like the thirsty ground after a short cloud burst.

The almost-full moon cast a silvery glow over her high, rosy cheekbones and full mouth. Wisps of dark, glistening curls floated around her head like a prairie nymph surrounded by moonbeams.

"How come you stopped giving me piggyback rides?" she asked, sadness coloring her voice.

"What?" Where had that come from? And did he want

to answer her?

"How come you stopped giving me piggyback rides?" She evidently remembered the event, too. And with as much sorrow as he did.

Oh, boy.... What was he supposed to say?

Try the truth, bucko.

"You started growing." He'd watched her transform from a spunky little girl into a beautiful young woman.

"I started growing?" Skepticism laced her voice, tying a knot around his heart. "You can wrangle wild horses and herd frightened cattle, but you couldn't carry the weight of a thirteen-year-old girl?"

"You were turning into a woman, Molly. Right in front of my eyes. I started thinking and feeling things that no randy buck has any right to about a young girl." The crushed look on her face the first time he'd told her 'no' had just about killed him.

Her stunned comprehension rolled over him.

"I never realized."

Of course, she didn't. She was a naïve young woman in a siren's body and she had no idea what she did to his heart, much less his body.

The silence stretched out for a long moment.

"When did you stop wanting to marry me?" Dread sat in his stomach like a cold dumpling.

"I don't know. Tonight, I guess, when you were making plans without me." She slid off the boulder and took a few steps away. "For crying out loud, Zach, this is the first time I've seen you this close up or talked to you in months. All you do is work, work, work. And then all of a sudden it's just time to tie the knot. I don't even know you anymore."

"I don't have a choice, Molly. Your dad is too old to be running a spread this large. And I'm still just a ranch hand. I have to prove I've got what it takes to run this ranch and support you properly." Zach slipped off of the boulder and turned her to face him. Anger snapped in her brown eyes.

"That's all well and good. But you sure don't act like you want to marry me. You never even proposed. Just came up with some arrangement between you and Papa. And you sure as shootin' have never said you l—"

Zach grabbed Molly and fused his lips to hers. He couldn't let her pursue that line of thinking.

Sweet mother of Abraham Lincoln.

Pleasure galloped through him like a runaway horse. He wanted to tell her just how much he loved her, but the words stuck in his throat. If her papa found out he'd broken his end of the bargain...

Molly melted against him. His hands roamed her back, clutching her against him. Her plush breasts pressed against his chest. He couldn't help the low groan that rumbled from his throat into her mouth.

She yanked herself from his embrace, wiping a sleeve across her moist lips. "That's what you're really after, isn't it? Just someone to bed. That, and the ranch." Fear and dismay shimmered in her eyes.

"Hells bells, Molly. This place isn't worth everything I've been through in the last twenty-five months."

"Well, if that's the way you feel about it, then what are you still doing here?"

Chapter Three

Zach whirled away from her and stalked back to the homestead. He was no Jacob, but he'd work fourteen years if need be to have her. Why couldn't she see that? It didn't matter, though. She wanted to hear the words.

She needed to hear them. All her doubts would disappear, he was certain of it.

But his honor as a man of his word was at stake. Not only to Jed, but to Molly, too.

"Boy?" Jed Miller's voice carried across the ranch square from the back porch steps.

Zach stopped. Just what he needed. A riled-up father giving him what-for for breaking his little girl's heart. Wasn't like he wasn't partially to blame.

"I suppose you were presented a perfect opportunity to share yer feelin's and you didn't." The moon sharpened the wrinkles of the older man's face.

"That about sums it up." Zach hooked his thumbs into his waistband and stood stock-still waiting for the tongue-lashing.

"Boy, you have nine days to make her change her mind."

He hated it when Jed called him 'boy'. "The only thing that's going to make her change her mind is hearing me say that I love her."

"Let me tell you somethin', boy." Pain and bitterness strangled the old man's voice. "I told Molly's mother that I loved her every day, but she never believed me."

Zach nodded. He didn't know much about Belinda Miller; she was already sick when he'd come to the ranch. She'd passed on shortly after that, when Molly was eight. "But why? You always took such good care of her and Molly. Starting a cattle ranch is tough work, but from what I've heard, it didn't take you long to make it a success."

"It's not always the tellin' that convinces them. Oh,

they like to hear it, sure, but sometimes it's the backing it up with the showin' that proves it. I know you got it in you to tell her, son. Most men do. And it's not always the providin' for either. That's a man's job."

A deep-seated sadness stole across Jed's face. "It's the little things, Zach. It's time spent or a gift given. Not a house or horse, but a flower picked or a poem written, no matter how awful. That's what a woman needs. Things I never did for Belinda."

The few times Zach had seen her, Belinda Miller's face had been pinched and haggard. He thought it was her sickness. "Is that what this two-year deal was all about? Me trying to prove my feelings without saying the words?"

"Partly. But I wanted to see if you had it in you to work hard, dog-tired, bone-wearyin' hard. I don't have a son of my own and if I'm gonna pass the ranch on, I wanted to make sure you were... well, worthy. Not only of the ranch, but of Molly."

"And...?"

"You've done a fine job with the ranch, and until tonight I thought you were doin' all right with Molly. But, I guess she's been havin' some misgivin's about the whole thing."

"I thought she was just nervous about the wedding night."

"Well, I'm sure she is, but I imagine if she don't think you love her, like her ma claimed I didn't love <u>her</u>, then Molly'd not be wantin' to marry and experience that kinda sorrow and bitterness."

"I'm sorry it turned out that way for you, Jed." What more could he say? Jed nodded and turned into the house.

Maybe Zach just needed to stick with his horse. Ranger whinnied in greeting when he entered the barn. Ah, but a horse was no substitute for the love of a good woman. And Molly loved him. He was as certain of that as he was that the sun would rise. But how to convince her that he loved her, too?

A good, hard ride always put things in the right light. "How 'bout a midnight ride, fella?" Zach stroked the horse's smooth, dappled face. Ranger butted his nose against Zach's hand and he chuckled. "I know. It's been a

82

long time since we pulled an all-nighter. Let's go, boy."

Zach led Ranger from the barn and swung onto the animal's back, settling into the weathered saddle.

Lightning flashed in the distance, illuminating the huge thunderheads on the horizon. He'd have to keep an eye on the dark clouds and stay on high ground. He nudged Ranger to a trot. The high ridge on the northern edge of the ranch might be hiding a head or two of wandering cattle. Might as well be doing something useful while he was out there.

The loud, sharp crack of lightning rent through the night like a huge bullwhip.

Molly sat bolt upright, her heart pounding like her mare at full gallop. Thunder reverberated through the night, shaking the thick stone walls of the house.

Molly padded to the window and pulled back the curtains. Thoughts of Zach flashed through her mind, much like the lightning zig-zagging across the dark sky. Her insides felt battered as if she were standing in the tempest outside. She didn't know what to do. She loved Zach, she wanted to marry him, but she didn't want to be unhappy like her mother.

Nor did she want to be nothing more than a brood mare, or worse yet, used for only one thing.

A crisp night wind rushed in, raising goose bumps on her arms and legs. Dropping the curtain, she crawled back into bed.

Molly awoke to shouts and whinnies coming from the yard. What on God's green earth was going on so early? Had the rooster even crowed yet? She slid out of bed and looked out the window. The hired hands led their saddled horses into the ranch square.

"There's no tellin' which way he mighta gone. The storm washed away any tracks he mighta made," Calvin called to the others. "We'll have to split up."

Coldness gripped her and the back of her neck tingled.

Zach.

Molly grabbed her heavy wrapper and raced downstairs. Papa was already in the saddle. "Papa, what's happened?" She clutched his dusty boot.

"Zach's missin'." Papa pulled away from her. "Get back inside, girl. There's nothing you can do."

The men scrambled onto their mounts, and separated themselves into two groups.

"No, wait. He went that way." She pointed toward the ridge to the northeast of the homestead. "I saw someone heading out last night. It must've been Zach."

Papa nodded. "You heard her. It's a start. Let's go."

Chapter Four

The men left hours ago. And another summer storm had blown through. Molly paced from one end of the wraparound porch to the other. The low rumblings of thunder echoed her constant plea.

"Please bring him home safe. Please bring him home safe. Please bring him home safe."

"Come, Mijita," said Carmen, their housekeeper, for about the tenth time. "Come eat a biscuit or something."

She couldn't. Fear gnawed at her stomach like a rat on a bag of feed. If she ate, it would sit like a rock at the bottom of her stomach, or she'd throw it back up.

Another roll of thunder began. But this time it was different. She cocked her head, listening. It sounded like a stampede. Only it wasn't cattle, it was horses.

She flew around the house and down the steps to the ranch square, where the riders were sliding off their lathered mounts.

"We found him. Haney went to fetch the doc. We need to get ready for him," Jonesy said.

"Calvin, Red, and yer pa are bringing him in. He hit his head and busted a leg. Hain't came to yet, when I took off," Carlos said.

Oh, God, please help him.

She fetched everything she thought the doc might need and took it to the bunkhouse. She put fresh bedding on Zach's bunk and then waited.

And waited. She paced again, up and down the length of the main room of the bunkhouse, unable to stand still. Sweat trickled down her back.

The noise of the search party reached her and she hurried outside.

Zach's limp body hung over Calvin's lap, his left leg twisted at a terrible angle, his denim pants bloody.

The doctor's wagon wheeled to a stop moments later and Haney reined his horse to a halt right behind him.

The doc jumped from his seat and both men ran to Calvin's mount to help Zach down.

A groan tore from Zach's throat when they moved him and Molly jumped out of her skin.

His face was so pale. And his head was bloody. Oh, God, please don't let him die.

They carried him as carefully as a bunch of rowdy cowpokes could, which was surprisingly gentle, and laid him in his bed.

The doctor stitched the gash in his head and then, with the help of the hired hands, yanked his leg back into position. Zach cried out, even in his unconscious state. Molly could barely stand it for him. Her heart broke at his pain.

Papa shooed her out of the bunkhouse once the doctor was finished so the men could clean him up. She hated to leave him, if only for a second. He could've died and it would've been all her fault.

Molly looked up when Papa came into the bunkhouse one evening several days later.

"How's he doin'?" Papa stood at the door.

She shrugged. "I don't know, for sure. Fine, I guess. There's been no change."

"He's a good man."

She gazed at Papa. "That was never in question." And in the dim light of Zach's bunkroom, her papa's age penetrated her heart. And how hard Zach worked to carry that burden no matter what the reason. At least, she could be grateful for that.

"He'll do right by you, Daughter."

"I wanted more than being done right by, Papa." Was it too much to ask?

"I know you do, girl." His voice, soft and sad, drifted away as he turned and left.

But she would settle for it. Almost losing Zach was the worst thing she'd ever been through, aside from Momma dying.

She loved him, and suddenly she couldn't imagine life without him. Even if that meant marrying him and him not loving her back.

His words from the night on the boulder came back to

her. How her maturing body had affected him. And how he'd cared enough about her to keep his distance although it hurt her feelings terribly at the time.

A low murmur snagged her attention. Zach's body twitched and squirmed under the sheet. The laudanum was wearing off.

"But I love her, Jed." His voice was low and rough from disuse.

Molly stopped in mid-stand and looked at him. Did she really just hear that? Maybe her mind was playing tricks on her. She'd been willing him to wake up for three days. Her heart took off at a mad gallop.

His eyes remained closed, and his head moved restlessly from side to side. "Molly, please... love you... marry me..."

She dropped back into her chair. Dare she believe the drugged-up ramblings of a wounded man? She didn't know.

He continued to thrash and moan, so she gave him another dose of the medicine and soon he rested quietly.

Molly took his hand and pressed her tear-streaked cheek against it. "I love you, too," she whispered.

"How's our patient?" Doc asked the next day, setting his bag on the rough wooden table, paying his daily visit.

"He's still unconscious, I guess. But he spoke last night when the laudanum started to wear off."

"You don't say?" The doc looked pleased. "That's good. Means he's probably not in a coma. It's just the drug keeping him out."

"About what he said...he wouldn't lie, would he?"

The doc raised a bushy gray eyebrow. "He probably couldn't lie. It's not truth serum or anything, but his mind is in such a relaxed state that it's near impossible. Lying takes scheming, and right now, he isn't capable of that."

She nodded. Okay, so Zach did love her. But why wouldn't he just tell her?

"We probably ought to keep him dosed up for another day. I'll come by again tomorrow afternoon. Just give him small doses from mid-morning on so that I can try to catch him coming out of it to figure out how much pain he's in."

***

The brisk breeze ruffled Molly's dark curls, swirled amongst the wedding guests, and sent the vivid gold, rich burgundy, and bright green leaves chattering and shimmering in the dazzling fall sunshine. Much as she enjoyed the pine-scented smoke from the huge bonfire, Molly preferred the delicious scent of her husband-to-be. He smelled of sunshine and horses and leather.

The ranch hands stood in a semi-circle on one side of the bride and groom, while the folks from town surrounded them on the other side. Reverend Stanley concluded the ceremony. "I now pronounce you man and wife. You may kiss the bride."

With a finger to her chin, Zach tilted Molly's face up. His eyes darkened a shade as he leaned in to kiss her. Her heart soared. She no longer feared that look and all that it promised.

"I love you, Molly Rafferty, until the day I die," he whispered as his lips touched hers.

Chapter Five

Molly stretched as awareness stole over her. Good night, her body ached all over. Had her feather ticking turned into rocks overnight? And what was that awful high-pitched noise?

Oh, no...

Her eyes popped open and her gaze darted around the room. Her family pictures hung in a haphazard pattern on the wall over the sofa. The lamp still burned, but the hot chocolate was no longer hot. Evidently she'd spent the night in her armchair.

Sadness and disappointment settled over her like the heat of a Texas summer. She stood on unsteady legs and staggered to her room to shut off the annoying alarm. How she missed the sound of the rooster crowing at five o'clock.

The hot shower eased the aches and kinks out of her knees and back. One of the only things she recalled missing while she was in Texas. The cup of yogurt and crunchy granola bar she choked down paled in comparison to the fluffy scrambled eggs, thick, crispy bacon, and dense biscuits laden with freshly churned butter Carmen served. Not even IHOP could compete.

She drew the thick draperies open and caught her breath. The pristine whiteness reflecting off the snow-covered street below startled her. She'd been wishing for the muted colors of a dusty Texas prairie. She sighed and leaned her head against the freezing pane. The street below had been plowed and people were starting their day. She had to change her clothes. She certainly wasn't dressed for Omaha in January.

Peering out the glass doors of her apartment building, Molly inspected the sidewalks. Shoveled and sanded, just the way she liked them, at least in winter. She tightened her scarf, buttoned her outer jacket, and stepped out. The icy air scratched her nose and throat.

Her cheeks prickled from the thirty-something temperature. A brisk walk would do her good, though. She probably gained a few pounds while she was in Texas, what with all those hearty meals she'd consumed.

She shook her head. Come on, Molly—get a grip. You weren't really in Texas.

No. And while she could live without the Texas heat, a good man didn't seem too much to ask for.

The accountant's office where she worked was a couple of blocks away, but she liked the walk. She considered it forced exercise. That, and she liked the historic architecture of the buildings in the Old Market.

A door opened ahead of her, blocking her path, but there was no sand where she stepped. With a thud and a soft "ooph" she landed on her backside.

"Oh, I'm so sorry, Miss. Are you all right?"

A tingle shivered through her. She knew that voice, but it couldn't be. She hadn't hit her head. And she was pretty sure she was awake and in the correct time zone, time line, whatever. Looking up into a memorable pair of gray eyes, she gasped.

The cowboy hat-and-booted man dropped his worn leather satchel and helped her to her feet. "Molly? Molly Miller?"

"Yes..." It couldn't be. A whiff of cologne drifted her way and she closed her eyes. How on God's green earth did they manage to bottle the smell of laundry soap, hard-working man, and sunshine?

"It's me, Rafe. Rafe Zachary from back home." A wide, bright smile broke across his face. The one that always made her stomach flip-flop. Even when it wasn't directed at her.

Oh. My. Gosh. Captain of the football team and the debate club, and the hottest and nicest guy in school. She'd had a crush on him since the sixth grade. She hadn't put two and two together, but no wonder Zach had seemed so familiar. And no wonder she'd been instantly smitten.

"What're you doing in Omaha?" she asked. Great, Molly. That was brilliant. She hoped he'd chalk up the blush she felt rushing over her cheeks to the just-over-freezing temperature and not her acute sense of embarrassment and pleasure.

"I'm in town on business, working on a deal with ConAgra."

"ConAgra?" Only one of North America's largest packaged foods companies. Wow.

"Yep. I inherited a cattle ranch in Tex—"

Molly wobbled and he grabbed her arms to steady her, the heat of his gloved hands burning through her parka.

"Molly, are you okay?"

Nodding, she opened her eyes and offered him a weak smile. "I'm okay. You just surprised me, that's all." Where were Mulder and Scully when you needed them?

"Hey, listen, I'm going to be in town a few more days. I'd like to make up for my carelessness by taking you out to dinner."

"That's really not necessary, Rafe." She pinched herself to make sure she wasn't still dreaming.

"Then you don't want to have dinner?"

Dare she hope that was disappointment flashing through his eyes? "I'd love to have dinner. But for the sake of having dinner, not because you feel you have to atone for something."

"Great." He smiled again as he reached into the pocket of his fur-lined, denim jacket and pulled out a business card. "Call me this afternoon after three and I'll get your address. My cell number's on there." The tumbleweed that was her stomach bounced down the street and around the corner.

She was going out to dinner with Rafe Zachary.

She was going out to dinner with Rafe Zachary.

She was going out to dinner with Rafe Zachary.

If anyone suggested that she'd ever go out to dinner with Rafe Zachary she'd have laughed in their face.

When she opened the door that evening, he stood there in a charcoal gray suit, his bright blue tie embossed with silver spurs.

He held out a perfect long-stemmed yellow rose. "You look lovely."

His eyes reflected his sincerity. It sure wasn't love. And it wasn't quite desire, but it was close. And she'd take it.

At least for now.

He held her coat for her and settled his hand at her back as they walked to the elevator. She liked the feeling it gave her. Of being cherished and important. Special.

"So, have you ever been to Texas?"

Molly laughed. "Funny you should ask."

About the Author

Jen FitzGerald lives in Fort Worth, Texas with her husband, three children, and two dogs. She has one completed manuscript, three works-in-progress, and three other stories on the plotting board. An active member in her local RWA chapter, North Texas Romance Writers of America, Jen is currently serving her second term as the 2007 & 2008 President. More about her and her work can be found at www.propg.com/jenfitzgerald.

A Lady in Deed

by

Nikki Hollaway

Dedication

To my two favorite cowboys, James and Hunter.

To Katrina and Wes, thanks for reading...
and then reading it again.

You guys made this possible.

Texas, 1877

Porcelain exploded against the wall sending tiny shards flying out like shot from a scatter gun with a fierceness that surprised even her. The youngest of the Granger boys winced slightly as the piece of china flew by his face but otherwise remained stoic and, if she read his slow nod correctly, bored by her behavior.

Havenleigh Pettit could only take comfort in the fact her aim had been a tad off. True, the man deserved worse, but a teacup to the eye would have been too quick. Instead, she bit her lip trying to hold back the smile as her fingers brushed against the matching saucer.

If he was taking it all she'd be damned if it was in anything short of a thousand pieces.

"Are you through?" Brayden said as he stepped toward her, readjusting the weathered brim of his black cowboy hat.

"Get out of my house!" Haven reared her hand back and the tiny plate sailed through the air, shattering against the wall, but not before grazing his left cheek.

A gloved hand rose to shield his face from further attack. "Ma'am, seeing I am now the rightful owner of everything in this here kitchen, I'm gonna have to ask you to stop breaking my dishes."

"Go to hell, Granger." Haven screamed as the billowing anger overwhelmed her. She knew her rage needed to be directed at her brother, after all this was his fault to begin with, but it was Brayden Granger standing before her now taking too much pleasure in delivering the bad news.

"Miss Pettit, I'm only claiming what's rightfully mine." Brayden lifted the deed out of his breast pocket and held it between two fingers as he motioned for her to take it. When she refused to move he returned it to his pocket. "I've been more than generous offering to pay your way to anywhere you need to go. Hell, I even gave you twenty-five days to take what you wanted, but you refused both offers. Now your time is up and my patience is wearing thin."

She knew Brayden spoke the truth. She had no legal right to defend her home. Her brother had staked her family's livelihood, lost, and ran off leaving her high and dry, just like he'd always done. However, this latest trouble Lucas had gotten them into was one hell of a tangle, and she had no idea how to get out from under this one.

Although Haven knew she should cherish what little family she had left, she despised her brother with a passion. She hated him for always leaving her to deal with his messes. She hated his frivolous ways after Papa's death. But most of all she hated the way he had ridden out of Coldwater a month ago after losing with a pitiful straight everything their papa had bled and toiled for. And lost to a Granger at that! Rumor had it the cur-dog had ridden clean out of Texas just to avoid her. He need not worry; she had a full place-setting waiting for him when he returned.

"I suppose I should welcome you with open arms, huh?" Haven retorted with thick sarcasm. "Offer you a cup of coffee to go alongside everything else I own."

"I don't want a cup of anything from you." He quipped as he rubbed his reddening cheek. He then continued with a quietness which did nothing but draw concern from her. "You have no idea what the other terms of the wager were, do you?"

She had lost her home—that much she knew—but Lucas had left before he had told her anything. Haven had never been one for surprises and by the way Brayden's gray eyes narrowed, she knew she was in for something unpleasant.

He stood there like a slate of cool granite. There was no emotion, none of the smugness one would expect from a man with the upper hand. He then shook his head, almost as if in pity.

Haven stiffened. How dare this man pity her. She was a Pettit, strong and proud. No matter the adversity, she always prevailed. As much as an inconvenience as Brayden Granger had become, Haven promised herself

98

she'd see this ordeal through to the end.

He answered his own question, this time more to himself than directed at her. "Of course not. If your brother had told you anything you wouldn't still be here."

"What could be worse than being thrown out of the only place I've ever lived?" She scoffed as she casually plucked the thick leather bound volume of *Wooldrift's Text of Practical Botany* from the bookcase and held it in her arms. Cradling her mama's book against her chest, she waited for the unpleasant revelation.

"The terms. Lucas laid down the deed to the land and *everything* on it."

Haven stared him down, squeezing the book closer in uneasy fear. Did he mean what she thought he meant?

"Miss Pettit, your brother drained the pockets of every man looking to bluff a win at that table. So yes, you could be worse off than with me."

"What are you talking about?"

"He dickered *you* away, and on a lousy hand at that."

Haven panicked; had young Granger come to claim his scandalous win? No, this can't be happening, not even Lucas could've been so immoral to ante his own blood.

An overdue smug smile creased his lips. "Is Haven Pettit for once rendered speechless?"

She breathed in one long, deep, angry breath. Hundreds of pain-inducing acts she so desperately wanted to attempt on Brayden cluttered her thoughts. However, as his towering frame overshadowed her she thought of a better idea. She calmed herself as she called his bluff. "I'm not property, and I happen to know slavery has been abolished for some years now, so I'm not part of any deal."

Brayden shrugged nonchalantly. "You're welcome to stay."

"I will not play harlot in some perverse fantasy of yours."

He chuckled. "Don't you worry. I don't intend to collect in that way, but I will be taking everything else." He removed his hat. His unfashionably long dark chestnut hair spilled over his eyes as he sat, propping his feet up on her sawbuck table.

She ground her teeth at his flippant dismissal. She may not be the most ladylike woman in Coldwater but...what the hell was she thinking? Why did she even give a damn how Brayden Granger felt about her?

He looked distraught as he ran his hand through his hair, pushing the strands away from the week's worth of dark stubble. Watching him she knew exactly what had sparked her newfound panic. She was angered at her own traitorous attraction to the roughrider in her kitchen.

Seated, he was less intimidating and almost looked tired. The air was tense around them as his feet dropped to the floor, his cowboy boots tapping a quick pulse on the puncheon floorboards. He sat there silent as he fidgeted with the scattered dried yellow petals near the center of the table. He crushed the thin parchment skins between his thumb and forefinger before brushing them onto the floor.

She grabbed his wrist as he reached for another. "Please, stop that."

They both locked eyes, neither one shifting their gaze. Haven swallowed as her fingers released the grip on his hand. She backed away, hesitant of his reaction.

His silver spurs continued to jingle a tempo her heart seemed to follow. "Where else would you go? What kind of man would I be if I turned you out to the wolves?"

"You are too kind." She forced the sarcasm in her voice. What was wrong with her? She should not fear this man. She should not feel...oh, god what were these feelings she felt towards him? What matter of emotion could cause her heart to race and settle in her throat?

"I need help running the ranch anyway. Just don't expect a wage." He maintained his stare, awaiting an answer. Her knees trembled and she quickly looked away, her cheeks flushed at her reaction. His deep voice pulled her back. "Haven? Are you ill?"

"I'm fine!" She shot back. *Get a hold of yourself*, she ordered silently.

"If King hadn't been in the saloon that night I would've never taken your brother's ridiculous wager, but you know my father has been after your land for years. If I hadn't played the hand to win, one of my brothers, or some other low-life drifter looking to gain quick pleasure, would have. So, although I understand this might not be your most favorable position, I guaran-damn-tee you no one else would have been as lenient as I've been."

Damn him for pointing out his redeeming qualities. She did not need this. He was enticing already. Haven had always fancied the youngest of the Granger boys, and now his pleasant tone was not only flustering her more, it was also ruining her tantrum.

She had to admit, he had been as gentlemanly as one could be while throwing someone off their own homestead. A few weeks ago, he had even offered to pay her fare back to her aunt's in Boston, but that was not the point. He was taking her home.

Reluctantly, Haven swallowed back her pride; he had made a valid argument, and neither one of them was leaving. Perhaps they could agree to some kind of arrangement, at least for the time being. "Am I now supposed to lay my graces at your feet?"

He eyed her cautiously. "Not throwing that book at my head would be a sufficient 'yes and thank you'."

She glanced down at the heavy book in her arms and carefully placed it back in its proper spot on the shelf. What was his angle? Haven knew the reputation of Brayden Granger. He was nothing more than a glorified vigilante doing his father's bidding. Haven knew what he lacked in experience, in comparison to the rest of the brood, he surely made up in reflexes. He was quick on the draw and short on temper. Which made one hell of a deadly combination. This made no sense; why was he here now offering to run her ranch? Yes, what *was* Brayden Granger's angle?

"What's your stake in working the ranch? You're far from a rancher. I know it, you know it, and hell, everyone in a fifty-mile radius knows it. Face it; you ain't the settling down type."

He shrugged again as he picked at the stale bread lying on the table. "I won it."

"It just seems logical to give the land to your fath—"

"This is mine. My father has nothing to do with my ranch, no matter how much he bellows. It may be only a few cattle now..."

"Six." Haven sighed, almost embarrassed to admit the small number of steer left grazing on the land. She didn't dare tell him those numbers were dwindling by the day.

His brow crinkled. "Six head?" Brayden exhaled slowly. "Well, like I said, it may be a few cattle now, but I plan to build this ranch back up to it's former glory."

"Are you drunk?" Did this man not see the shambles the ranch had become? Cattle disappeared by the handful and she was the only person willing to set foot on the land lately.

"It's nine in the morning." He glared, seemingly offended by her question. "No, I am not drunk but I sure as hell should be. You Pettit's always sound more rational after a few."

If he wasn't talking through a liquored haze Haven knew Brayden must have some other assurance behind his farfetched aspiration. She tilted her head in slight intrigue. "How much money *did* you win?"

"Enough."

****

Brayden watched her shovel the stall in silence. Surprisingly, it had been difficult ordering the girl around, especially when the damn woman took such pleasures in telling *him* all the things *he* was doing wrong. In the three days he'd been on the Lazy L Ranch he'd bitten his tongue a dozen times and clenched his fist until his knuckles paled white a dozen more.

Had he been a single ounce less a gentleman he'd.... No, Brayden knew in the end things needed to be done and the two of them needed to work together. As much as it raked his chaps he was glad she actually knew how to run a ranch, because he didn't know a damn thing when it came down to it.

King had groomed his two eldest brothers, Seth and Heath, to take over the family's ranch. Brayden's responsibilities had been to keep his target practice out of earshot, although he frequently failed in that causing startled cattle to stampede on many occasions.

This cooperative arrangement of working the ranch side-by-side had been trying for them both—although he was pretty sure it bothered proud Haven much more than it did him.

The Lazy L Ranch had once rivaled King's, but after Lowell's death two years ago and Lucas' lack of propriety the Lazy L had waned down to a glimmer of what it once had been. Everyone could tell Haven had tried her damnedest to make it work but there were too many forces pushing her to fail.

After the land feud started six years ago—when the Red River shifted, cutting into the Granger range and giving the Pettit's a few extra acres to graze—King had systematically begun to drain the competing ranch's profits. The cattle thefts and the slim number of hands willing to work against the King Ranch were just a few of his father's doings. Now King wanted it all, and without Haven's brother or father to protect it, Brayden knew it'd only be a matter of time before he took it.

He cinched tight his horse's girth strap as he prepared the old gray mare for a survey ride. Of course, that was if he ever made it outside the stable. Brayden couldn't stop watching her. He'd never thought of Haven as anything more than the smart-ass kid next door sporting the temper of a caged wildcat. He'd admired her spunk and most of all Brayden enjoyed watching his father squirm every time she refused to back down. But now she had blossomed into something more and even he would be a fool not to see the woman she'd become.

Her long brown hair was braided at the nape. It bounced like an alluring pendulum against the soft mound of her behind as she walked. Even in dirty trousers and with her face caked in mud—and only god knew what else—Haven Pettit was one helluva sight. Her beauty was unconventional, natural.

That's what had kept his interest; Haven was different, independent and full of the wild spirit that could transform any sound man into a love-starved puppy. How else could he explain his strong desire to make this woman, a Pettit, proud of him?

The sound of approaching horses drew his attention away from Haven and back into reality. Leading his mount from the stable, he shaded his eyes from the midday sun as he watched the three men ride closer. He recognized his brothers immediately. King had begun his hostile takeover.

Seth, the eldest of the brothers, motioned for the others to stop. "Well, if it ain't our baby brother playin' big boss."

"What do you want?" Haven demanded as she stepped up behind Brayden.

"*Woowee,* boys!" Heath Granger, the second eldest, hollered. "Would you look at Brayden. He flew big daddy's nest only to feather his own with that purdy piece. You want to keep all the fun to yourself. Now how fair is that?"

Haven started toward the men on horseback. "Why don't you get off my land?"

"Haven." Brayden warned as he held her back by the excess fabric of her work shirt. He knew Haven could handle herself but something told him Seth, Heath, and Cody weren't here on a social call.

"We just came to see what we're missing." Seth slid off his horse and started walking toward Haven, looking her up and down. "I bet with a little soap, she'd clean up real nice." He reached out to stroke her face but she pulled back as if the man was contagious.

Brayden knew Seth was accustomed to getting whatever he wanted and his displeasure in Haven's knee-jerk reaction was evident.

"Don't you ever touch me—" Haven rebutted before Brayden quickly stepped in between her and his brother, cutting her off before her hellcat temper could flare.

"Baby brother, you need to control your property. Speaking of which, keep your pitiful herd off our land or they may go missing."

The other two brothers chuckled.

"They won't cross the Red. Don't worry." She added matter-of-factly.

Seth turned to Haven. "Shut that mouth of yours, or I swear I'll make good use of it."

Heath piped in, still atop his palomino. "Who said anything about the river? The Red runs clean through our land. Didn't you hear? King reclaimed his acres."

"You can't do that. The river has always been the boundary. You can't cut us off from the river." She continued despite Brayden's sharp glares of warning.

"Who's the boss, you or her? Really, Brayden, she's pushing my patience."

"Haven, quiet." Brayden demanded. He looked at the

other boys still mounted. He began to grow uncomfortable as he noticed them eyeing her like a salivating pack of wild dogs. "How am I to water my herd?"

"Ain't our problem, now is it?"

****

He was still considering the problem as he lay on the uncomfortable bed. He had given Haven the house. It didn't feel right putting her in the drafty bunkhouse, but it also didn't feel right sleeping under the same roof. So, *he* spent the nights in the bunkhouse.

The distance between them at night also aided in suppressing the urges she worked up in him during the day. Not once in his twenty-five Aprils had a single woman driven his head crazy whilst driving his body wild at the same time. Havenleigh Pettit was a force this Texan had never before reckoned with.

A noise outside pricked his senses and he sat up in his bunk. He listened harder, trying to hear over the night's hum of croaks and crickets. Quickly slipping into his trousers he made his way to the main house. From the outside everything seemed in order. Perhaps it had just been a delirious product of exhaustion mixed with his imagination.

As he approached the porch he noticed the front door was ajar. Then he heard it again, the shrill scrape of wood against wood, like furniture being drug across a room. Bounding up the porch steps Brayden pushed open the door. His hands immediately went to his waist holsters but were instead met with emptiness. Damn, he had left his hardware in his haste to dress.

Taking the stairs two at a time he rushed toward Haven's room. When he reached the top of the stairs he listened for a second before deducing the house was silent. There was no sign of trouble.

The bedroom door was shut, and for a moment he felt ridiculous standing outside her room half dressed, like an overzealous sentry. He turned to head back downstairs but a muffled cry sent him into action.

When the door didn't budge Brayden slammed into it with his shoulder. He felt the heavy object blocking his entrance scoot back from the doorframe, inch by inch. With one last shoulder ram, the door opened wide enough for him to squeeze into the room.

A large figure straddled Haven, pinning her down to the bed. A strong surge of rage coursed through his veins as he flew at her attacker.

In the darkness, Brayden tackled the man, not even wondering whether or not the intruder had been armed. All he knew was he had to protect Haven. Pulling the man to the ground Brayden pounded away without mercy.

"Brayden!" A tiny voice screamed.

His focus had been so deep into his rage he, for a second, had forgotten Haven was still in the room. He glanced up at the bed. She was sitting up crying, clutching her blanket at her chest as the fear inked her face. He looked down at the man bloodied at his feet; it was Seth.

When he saw the pain in her eyes, he could not measure the anger welling within him. He grunted and continued to swing, trying to destroy his brother with each crushing blow. Seth, curled in a ball to protect his body, was drunk beyond function. The strong stench of whiskey permeated the air as Brayden's fist fell with sickening thuds.

He yanked the colt from Seth's holster then stood and directed the barrel at his brother's temple.

"Brayden, no!" Terror now rattled her voice. It took a moment for him to realize *he* had caused her fear and not the man nearing death on the floor.

Brayden lowered his aim. The full moon streamed in her room, illuminating her wide eyes as she stared down at him, his knuckles raw and covered in another man's blood. Seeing Seth unconscious and unthreatening he remembered what was now important.

"Haven?" Brayden leaned in to comfort her, but she pulled away. "It's okay, I'm here. Are you all right? He hurt you any?"

She shook her head as her face fell on his shoulder. Her body racked in sobs. "Please, don't leave me."

"I'm not going anywhere. I promise."

****

"Can you wait here?" Brayden asked Haven as they stood outside the marshal's office. "I'll just be a moment."

Reluctantly she nodded; she had not left his side

since last night. She felt empty. Only he could comfort and protect her. The incident kept replaying itself over and over in her head. The feel of Seth's clammy hands pressing down over her mouth, holding her down so she could not move. The smell of alcohol on his breath as he bent to kiss her. *Oh, the vile taste of him.* Her stomach churned at the memory.

She wanted nothing more than to wash every grimy inch he had touched on her body, to cleanse herself of the memory of Seth Granger.

For the first time since Lucas left, she felt vulnerable. She had been a woman living alone and, although she knew the dangers, she had never felt frightened to be alone until now. *My god, what would have happened if Brayden hadn't been there...?*

Haven pulled her shawl tighter around her shoulders. A woman across the street walked into the general store alone as if the evils of the world had not yet scarred her. Another lady with her daughter strolled down the walkway.

Haven wanted to scream out to them and warn them of the dangers lurking in the shadows. She hated the fear placed upon her; she hadn't bargained for this. She had only wanted to keep her life, her home and her memories of her childhood. But it all had been marred in an instant by Seth Granger.

The mother and daughter made their way toward her. Haven glanced down at her faded calico as they neared in their more fashionable butternut dresses. The mother whispered to her daughter and they both snickered as they passed. The daughter turned back and sneered, baring her gnarled teeth and wicked venom. "Granger whore."

****

There was only silence between them that night at supper. She had been mulling the day over in her head. It was true, she had chosen to stay on, but those ugly words from town had haunted her all day. What had she expected to come about with this arrangement? She was living alone with a man with a slanted reputation without a chaperone. There were always repercussions that came with choices. Perhaps she deserved last night as much as she deserved the harsh speculation.

She sighed. She knew what she needed to do. Tomorrow she would send a telegram to Boston. She didn't want to leave. These past few days had been a whirlwind of emotions. Brayden Granger churned feelings within her body she never knew existed and now feared losing. She had always been attracted to his secret and nomadic ways, but only from afar. He had been her forbidden fruit. But even too much sweet nectar caused a bellyache.

She could no longer stay.

"What's the matter? You haven't said two words since the ride back, which for you is highly unusual."

"Nothing." Haven spoke carefully. She had no intentions of bringing him into her problems. "I'm just tired."

"Don't lie to me."

That wasn't a lie. She hadn't slept all night, and by the looks of Brayden's heavy eyes, neither had he.

She inhaled deeply. She was only putting off the inevitable. "I'm leaving on the next stage eastward. My aunt has three kids who I can help look after. Boston isn't too terrible."

"What are you talking about? This is your home."

"This is no longer my home. It's yours, and I can't do this anymore." Haven brushed the tears from her cheeks with the open palm of her hand. She hadn't wanted to cry, especially not in front of Brayden. She hated showing him her true emotions. She was supposed to be stronger than this, a proud Pettit. "I don't belong out here. I never have. I kept this ranch going for the memory of my ma and pa, but now there are only empty and lonely memories I'd rather soon forget."

"The Haven I know never gives up, no matter what. What's changed?"

"What's changed?" Haven sputtered. "Last night changed everything. The stupid wager changed everything."

"What would you say if I told you I don't want you to go?"

"I'd say you're crazy. The only reason you're holding on to this ranch is because of your ridiculous pride. Admit defeat. I have. Give the land to your father, so we can both move on. You don't need me here."

"I want you. It's not a matter of needing you." He whispered. She looked up into his eyes as the fire from the hearth flickered in their reflection. She saw Brayden's jaw clench. "Stay."

What was he asking of her? Was he that selfish? He could very well hire a dozen men to help him work the ranch. Could he not see it was a hard enough decision to leave her home?

Pulling the shawl across her shoulders she broke through the stillness of the room. "I need air."

Haven walked to the door and pulled it shut behind her. Even though the sun was fading fast the beauty of the flowers were still visible from the porch. Her fingers trembled as she caressed the soft petals in her mama's garden. Why did Brayden fluster her so? What was it about him that vexed every one of her senses?

Haven heard the front door close, but she wasn't in the mood to be around people, especially him.

"Haven, the last thing I want to do is pressure you. I just really—" Brayden looked around the garden. "What are those? Are they..."

"Rosa foetida. My grandfather claimed the color symbolized jealousy." Haven smiled slightly, she had always been proud of mama's roses. "My grandfather was a botanist. When my ma was a young child he left to travel the world cataloging rare species of flowers. On his last trip to Persia he managed to pot a small plant of yellow roses and brought it back with him to Boston. Months went by and the plant just wilted and never bloomed. He spent years ignoring his family and the rest of his work trying to get this single plant to thrive.

"Even though my ma grew up hating the bush, when he died she began taking care of it. It wasn't until my ma and pa moved out here and she planted the roots in Texas clay that the yellow roses began to flower."

"I've never seen ones that color." Brayden lowered his nose to the roses.

"The flowers were a piece of her father, his heart, his desire and despite everything she wanted to always keep that alive. When she died, I promised to keep them blooming."

"That's why the ranch means so much to you. You want to keep your parents' memories alive."

"Pa loved his land, and ma loved her roses." Haven brushed off the back of her dress as she stood. She bit her lip. Leaving was going to be more difficult than she'd first thought. "I just didn't want to fail either of them. The ranch and my mama's roses are special to me."

He took her in his arms. She felt perfect against the warmth of his body. She wanted nothing more at this very moment than to be with him, but she knew she had to pull away. "Bray—"

"Haven." Brayden moaned. His lips brushing against hers as he spoke. "Stay."

Haven tried to pushed away; she needed to distance herself from his warmth. "I can't."

"These past few days have been the most intriguing days of my life. I don't know everything, but the one thing I do know is I've never felt this strongly for a woman. Stay with me and I promise to never let anything bad happen to you."

Haven finally relaxed in his arms. She felt so safe but she knew the truth. "You can't keep that promise."

"No, but I promise to be here for you." Brayden reached for a folded piece of paper tucked in the waistband at his back. He handed the document to her. "The deed. I'm giving you back the Lazy L. I had the land marshal transfer it all into your name; neither I, Lucas, nor my family will have any rights to it. Haven, I want to stay and help you work it, but only if you want me to."

"Brayden, I—"

"Shh." He placed a single finger on her lips, silencing her. "I don't want to know your answer right now. Just let me have this moment, tonight."

****

Although he had promised never to leave her side, Brayden needed to tend to one last important piece of business. As he rode the long path up to the King Ranch, he was determined to give Haven back all twenty-five acres of her home.

"Where's King?" Brayden asked as he stepped onto the porch. His brother tilted a nod in acknowledgment but

110

didn't answer. "I ain't leaving 'til I see him."

"He's been waiting for you to come crawling back with your tail between your legs." Cody looked up from the chair where he relaxed. One leg was slung over the armrest and the rest of him slouched back. He slid his knife through an apple, clipping a wedge of fruit between his lips as he grinned. "That was one hell of a beatin' you laid on Seth. Can't say he didn't deserve it though; I'm actually surprised someone ain't done it sooner. Brother, you never fail to amaze me. Standing up to Seth like that, that took balls."

"Where's King?" Brayden asked again.

"Office." Cody smiled, pointing the tip of his blade to the left as apple juice dripped down his chin.

Brayden didn't know what he was going to say. His father's office had always intimidated him, and now it seemed like the lion's den. He had no idea how his father would react, but this needed to be done. King needed to know he no longer had pull on his youngest son.

"Come to beg me to take that wasteland off your hands?" King stated without looking up from his ledger books as Brayden shut the door behind him.

"Actually, no." Brayden mustered his courage.

King raised his head. "Excuse me? Then why are you here?"

"I'm relinquishing all my inherited holdings on King Ranch. I have two thousand dollars; that and my stock is plenty enough." Brayden lifted the sack he had carried in with him.

Puzzlement washed over his father's face as King raised his nose at him. Brayden knew that look; it was the calm before the twister. "Enough for what?"

Brayden slammed the bank bag on his father's desk. "Everything. I want her land back, the stolen cattle, and I don't want to see Seth or any of the others on her property again."

King casually glanced through the bag. "Where'd you get this?"

"It doesn't matter. What matters is you and I are through. I want nothing more to do with this family."

"You'd give it all up, your own flesh and blood, for a skirt? I thought I raised you better."

"You did one hell of a job teaching your boys how to treat women like property—to take what they want, when they want it, and I will never forgive you for that."

"Yes," His father grinned. "Seth told me about the other night, about how you tried to beat him to death over that..." King hissed, "Pettit woman."

"I didn't just try. I had every intention of lodging a lead ball into his temple, but *that Pettit woman* stopped me. Next time I can promise you it won't end as pretty. You should be thankful she was there or you'd be down two sons."

"Don't tell me what I should be thankful about, boy. You're the one who's lacking perspective right now. Are you planning to do something stupid like marry that poor trash?"

"I can only hope one day Havenleigh Pettit can overlook my past and my family, and deem me worthy enough to spend the rest of her life with."

King shook his head. "Whipped fool."

"Do we have a deal?"

"You can have your river bank." King's breath quickened as his lips pursed. Brayden read the anger clearly. No one had ever successfully negotiated with King Granger. "And you're no longer my son."

Perhaps those last words should have stung more, a son disowned by his own father, but instead they were simply liberating. Brayden nodded. "Then it's settled."

****

He saw her as he approached the house. She was haloed in the light of morning. This was a new day for him and he could only pray she would spend it with him.

This day and every day until his last.

"Brayden, you're back." She rushed down the porch steps dressed in the calico he had grown to love. Her thick brown hair spilled over her shoulders in a cascade of rich curls. She had been crying; the evidence shown through her puffy eyes. "When I couldn't find you this morning I thought you had reconsidered. You didn't, did you?"

"Reconsider what?"

"My ranch." Haven lowered her stare, her voice naught but a timid whisper. "And us. I do want you to stay with me."

Brayden's jaw clenched with raw emotion. He never knew how much he'd needed to hear those sweet words until now. She stood there so perfect, so loving, so accepting.

There had been no regret in his decision to walk away from his family. "I can't promise you tomorrow will be easier, but I do know you can't have roses without the rain." He clasped her hand in his as he led her around to the back of the buckboard.

Amongst his meager belongings was one potted plant he had plucked from the Granger estate garden on his way out. The two thick rooted stalks twisted and intertwined up into one large red rose bush.

"They aren't as enchanting as your mother's yellows, but I hope every time you see these bloom, you can think of me and you."

She stood there, her hand covering her mouth. New tears welled in her eyes. He hoped this time they were happier than her last.

Haven nodded. "Only if we can watch them bloom together many times over."

He raised his chin, grinning. "What do yellow roses with red roses symbolize?"

"Happiness." Haven threw her arms around his neck. "Oh, Brayden, they're perfect."

No, the new day she had given him was perfect.

About the Author

Nikki Hollaway currently lives in Texas with her husband and son and is busy working on several full length historical romances. When she isn't writing Nikki enjoys honing in her culinary skills and camping under the bright Texas stars. Check out her website at www.nikkihollaway.com for news and updates.

Someone to Run To

by

Mary Malcolm

Dedication

To My Family:
Thank you for your patience,
your support and your understanding
about me being an unemployed crazy person.

Eva Martin reached down to tie the laces on her sneakers before she headed back out into the Texas sun. It was the weekend of the "Hotter Than Hell, Mad Hatter Dash" and she didn't want to end up splattered in the middle of the hot cement after tripping over her own laces. She looked into the mirror hanging lopsided on a pole inside the cool down tent and adjusted her hat over her short brown hair.

This was her fourth time taking part in the Dash. The only rules were that you had to run fast, and you had to wear some kind of hat. That was fine; Eva had been running since she was a little girl and the hat part was fun. Not to mention it kept the sun out of her eyes. The Dash was a charity event she had found out about shortly after her divorce. It made a nice diversion each year as it fell on the same week as her wedding anniversary. Or what used to be her wedding anniversary. It was almost as if she was running away from her past.

She adjusted her pink bonnet rimmed with dozens of sunflowers and one perfect yellow rose, and headed out into the heat.

"Hey, watch it," a voice drawled as she tripped over a cowboy boot.

She let her eyes meander slowly from the tip of the boot up the very attractive blue-jeaned leg and finally to the face of the man who had spoken to her.

"I'm sorry," she said in return, "but you shouldn't sit so close to the entrance. Don't you know we're all getting ready for the race?"

His lips curled into a lazy smile that threatened to pull Eva's thudding heart right out of her chest. His cheek had a peach pit of a dimple in it and that smile reached all the way up to his pool-water eyes. Much lighter than her own blue eyes. He pulled the cowboy hat off of his head and pushed back his black hair as he looked up at her.

"Well, Lady," he said in that same slow-as-molasses voice, "that's exactly what I'm doing too."

Eva shook her head to clear the endearing image of that dimple and responded, laughing, "You? You know that the race is starting in about five minutes, right? Don't you think you might want to change out of those ridiculous boots and into some proper running shoes?"

The smile faded slightly from his face and he leaned toward her. "I can run faster in my boots than you could ever run in those fancy sneakers of yours. You wanna place a wager on the race? Something friendly, just you and me?"

Eva was tired of men who thought they were somehow better than her. She was a great woman--no, a brilliant woman--and there was no reason for them to think that they could hold anything over her. It annoyed her that men in the central part of Texas, the hill country, seemed to all feel that they were somehow better than the women. This man with his cockiness and those ridiculous boots had another thing coming if he thought he was some how better than her. Much less that he could beat *her* in a race. She could outrace him with one foot tied to the other. An evil little smile tugged at the corners of her mouth. "I think that sounds like a mighty fine idea, mister," she said as she put her hand forward for him to shake it.

"Name's Baxter, Baxter Higgens."

"Eva Martin. Nice to meet you."

They shook hands as a voice sounded over the intercom letting the racers know that it was time to move to the starting line.

He's awfully tall, Eva thought as Baxter stood up from where he'd been sitting. She was a tall woman herself, or at least taller than average at five-seven, but this man had to be at least six-four. She knew that his height could give him some kind of advantage in the race, but then again, he was wearing those boots. She smiled again. No challenge here.

"So what's the wager?" she asked as they lined up shoulder-to-shoulder among the sea of runners. "What is it that you're going to give me when I run circles around you?"

Baxter grinned down at her, "When I win," he said in his sultry voice, "you'll agree to go to the dance with me tonight."

The dance. Every year the organizers held a barn dance to bring everyone back together after the race. Eva had never gone. Still, she knew she was going to beat him so it seemed like a fair wager.

"Take your places," the intercom sounded again.

"And when you lose?" Eva asked as she took her spot among the runners.

"Runners, take your mark," the announcer called over the intercom.

"If I lose, I'll agree to go with you," Baxter said as he tipped his hat to her.

"GO!"

Eva stood dumbfounded for a moment as the other runners took off. She gathered her wits about her and took off behind them. She ran, faster than she would normally run at the beginning of a race, and caught up with Baxter before he got too far. For a man in boots, he ran pretty smoothly. Eva was impressed in spite of herself.

"You know, I never agreed to that," she said as she moved alongside him. "I'm beating you today, and I'm not taking you to the dance tonight."

Baxter looked down at her as he steadied his pace. "Then I guess I had better win," he said as he shot ahead of her once again.

Eva took a deep breath and pushed forward. She caught back up to him pretty easily. "You're not winning," she said smugly as she stepped in front of him and raced ahead.

Baxter grinned. She was beautiful to watch from behind. In fact, he'd almost be willing to lose the race if for no other reason than to keep this side of Eva in his sights. Then again, why would he risk his chance of getting her to the dance? He had been trying to get Eva's attention since he first saw her three years ago. He had hoped that he would meet her at the dance and he could ask her out, but she didn't show.

Then the next year, same thing. He could always track her down in town, ask her out that way. But Eva Martin had built a reputation during her short time in Shady Grove. She had turned down every man that asked, and left them bleeding where they stood. No, he had to be different than all the others, and this was the only way to do it. He saw that the finish line was coming up quickly.

Baxter and Eva were clearly in front of all of the other runners, so he sped up just enough to be right behind her. "Looks like you might win," he shouted over the din of the cheering crowd.

"I figured so all along," Eva shot back. The finish line was right there. *Right...wait! No!* Baxter dashed past her and through the tape before she had a chance to reach it. He slowed down now, jogging, then to a walk. Eva couldn't believe it. She couldn't believe he had beat her, and in *boots*!

"So I'll see you there. Or should I pick you up?" Baxter drawled as he walked over to where she now stood.

"I don't go to the dance," she said.

"You agreed to our wager, Ms. Martin, and I don't think you're the kind of woman who's going to back down from a bet." He reached down and picked up a slightly trampled yellow rose. "I believe this was yours," he said, handing it to her.

Eva watched as Baxter walked off, surrounded by all the people congratulating him for his win. Then she looked at the rose that lay, trampled and broken, in her hand. She took off her bonnet and walked irritably to her car.

****

"Baxter Higgins? Are you sure it was Baxter Higgins?" Eva's friend Mandy asked as they sat drinking lemonade in her kitchen.

"I'm positive," Eva said emphatically. "I mean, how am I supposed to forget a name like that? Baxter."

Mandy shook her head. "Well, you may not have realized it," she began, "but you are possibly the most envied woman in all of Brown County right now."

Eva scoffed. "You realize how ridiculous you sound, right?" She stood and put her lemonade glass in the sink. "He's just a guy. What, he's rich or something?"

"Rich, good looking, available, goes to the Cowboy Church, loves his family...all the women want him, and

120

all the men want to be him. I can't believe you don't know about Baxter Higgins."

"Well," Eva said. "They can have him. I didn't like him."

Mandy laughed. "Oh yes you did," she said as she sashayed over to her friend. "If you had only seen your own face while you were talking about him. And the way you say his name. *Bax-ter*," she said in a sing-song voice.

Eva laughed. "Cut it out! Sure," she continued, "he was cute, but so is my Labrador. I'd be more tempted to dance with Sunshine than I would with a man as arrogant as Baxter Higgins."

Upon hearing her name, Sunshine looked up expectantly from where she had been sleeping by the kitchen door. Then she turned her head as she heard a sound outside and began barking. Eva peaked out of her lace curtains at the black car coming up her gravel driveway.

"Now what in the world," she began as a man stepped out of the car. He had a long white box and came right up to her door. "Whatever you're selling, Mister, you had best sell it elsewhere," she said before he could open his mouth.

"I have a delivery," the man said as he handed her the box. "For Ms. Eva Martin. That's you, right?"

She took the box and watched the man as he got back into his car and drove away. She shook her head. This had been a very strange day indeed.

"What is it?" Mandy asked excitedly from behind her.

Eva turned around, holding the long box. She opened the card that had been attached. "Sorry about earlier, see you tonight, B," it read. She lifted the lid and looked down at the most beautiful yellow rose she had ever seen. It took her breath away.

"Oh my," Mandy said as she took the note from Eva. "Well, you may not like him," she said, "but he sure seems to like you."

Eva felt a smile tug at the corner of her mouth. He was pretty handsome, and she could have taken a swim in those eyes of his. Maybe it wouldn't be so bad to see this man at the dance. She couldn't lead him on though; Eva had vowed after her divorce to not let another man into her life, and she wasn't about to break that vow now. She let her fingers reach forward to caress the rose petals softly before she shut the lid on the box.

****

Hours later Eva was still having trouble getting that rose out of her mind. She had begun wearing a rose in her bonnet two years ago when her parents passed away. Every year on their wedding anniversary, Eva's father had given her mother twenty-five perfect yellow roses. He'd said that two dozen just wasn't good enough for the woman he loved. He would lay one perfect rose on her pillow and have the others waiting for her in their kitchen by the time she woke up.

Eva missed them both, terribly. She had known that her mother was dying, and had been preparing for it. When her father passed away shortly after her mother, it was a shock Eva had not been prepared for. She took a deep breath and scooted deeper into the plush leather chair where she sat reading.

She had to stop thinking about the rose, and more importantly, she had to stop thinking about the man that had sent it to her. It was sweet, she gave him that. And thoughtful. She hadn't noticed when the rose fell out of her bonnet, so for him to notice, and give it back to her.... All the same. She sighed and laid her book down on her knee. She closed her eyes for just a moment.

"Darling," the man said softly as he reached his hand toward her, "I've been waiting for you my entire life."

"Oh, my love," Eva replied. "I have been waiting for you. I have dreamt about you, longed to feel you in my arms. Oh, kiss me."

Eva's long green dress flowed around her as she rushed down the curved staircase of Tara and toward the man waiting at the bottom. He pulled her into his arms, the metal from his uniform pressing hard against her bosom.

"My love," he said as he kissed her eyelids, then the soft place behind her ear. "My dream."

"Dream."

Dream, Eva opened her eyes to realize that she was still in her study, though the novel, "Gone With the Wind", had fallen off of her knee. She smiled. Rhett.

Baxter. She was no Scarlett, but their pride was the same. It was getting late, and she had never backed down from anything in her life. She had a dance to get ready for.

****

"Oh get down, turn around, go to town, boot-scootin' boogie."

Eva tried to tune out the sound of Brooks and Dunn as she swam her way through the sea of people. "Mandy!"

Eva saw her friend standing next to the concessions table and worked her way to her. "What am I doing here?"

"What?" Mandy asked. She was swaying her hips back and forth to the music, "Cadillac, black jack," she crooned in time with the music.

"Mandy!"

"Sorry," Mandy smiled at the cute guy standing just behind Eva. "What did you say?"

"I said, what am I doing here," Eva replied as the song came to an end. "Why am I here?"

"You're here because the cutest, most amazing guy in town asked you." She turned from Eva for a moment, "Oh, Harold," she said, waving the man over. "I want the next dance, okay?"

Harold tipped his hat to her as he heel-toed himself back into the crowd of people.

"Go," Mandy said as she handed Eva a beer. "Mingle."

Eva shook her head as Mandy twisted and turned her way toward Harold. She set the beer on the concessions table and looked around for anyone else she might know. The duo "Big and Rich" started pumping through the speakers and Eva smiled. She always loved this song. She wasn't a big fan of country music, but "Save a Horse, Ride a Cowboy" just had a certain ring to it.

She started walking around the room, looking for her own cowboy. Or at least she was assuming he was a cowboy. He had worn boots to a race, and kept his hat on tight the entire time he ran. She saw Frank Crawford instead.

"Frank," she called as she walked toward him, waving.

One look at Eva and Frank stopped his conversation

short and walked quickly in the other direction.

That's odd, Eva thought. Frank had asked her out just a few months ago, and sure, she turned him down, but that was no reason for him to react so strongly.

"I think you'll find that most of them act that way toward you."

Eva heard that same slow-as-molasses voice as he sidled up behind her. She could almost feel his breath on her neck; a shiver ran up and then back down her spine.

"Why is that?" she asked without turning around. She was afraid to turn around, just hearing his voice had left her feeling melty inside, like hot caramel was pooling in her middle.

"Seems you've broken a few hearts in this town," Baxter breathed into her ear as he placed his hands on her shoulders. "Thank you for coming tonight. I don't think I could have stood joining their ranks."

Eva got her senses back in spite of the tingle of his hands on her shoulders. "So you've never had a woman turn you down then?" Eva questioned as she moved to turn around.

"I've had plenty," he said, his hot voice searing through her, "but I couldn't have taken having you turn me down."

"Is that so?"

"Yes ma'am," he said as he began to move his hips slowly in rhythm to the next song. He moved his hands down her arms and placed them on her hips.

She began to move to his rhythm. Before she could stop herself, she leaned her head on his chest. It felt strange, but right. He took one of her hands in his and held it close to his chest as they swayed. Eva smiled in spite of herself. He felt warm, solid against her. The song was perfect, as well.

She began to think about her dreams, all of the things she had aspired to. But one thing was missing in her life. Why was she so afraid to love again? Why was it that the men in this town cowered when they saw her walking on their side of the street? Her divorce had been hell, but she survived. She was stronger now than ever, in fact. She inhaled Baxter, trying to memorize how he smelled. She wanted to remember this moment. She knew it wouldn't last, and as the song was coming to an end she felt sad that he was about to let her go.

One last breath, one last beat of their hearts together and the song was over. She stayed where she was a moment longer than needed, but then took a step away from him. "Baxter," she began.

"Wait," he drawled. "Wait right there. I have something for you."

She watched him walk away. He wore the same boots, but the hat was different, and the jeans. And now instead of the white T-shirt he had worn earlier, he wore a blue long sleeved shirt that fit him perfectly. She watched as he pulled a box out from under one of the tables. He turned around and walked back to her.

"I'm sorry about what happened to your rose earlier," he said softly as he handed her the box.

"You didn't have to," she began as she took the box from him, "I mean, you sent one to my house, you didn't even need to do that."

"I wanted to," he said. He held his breath as Eva lifted the white lid and he watched the tears come to her eyes.

"What is it?" he asked, afraid he had done something wrong. He had waited too long to get this woman into his arms; his heart beat faster at the thought he might have ruined it all.

"How many roses are in here?" she asked softly. She leaned her face in to inhale the heady scent, then she looked back up at him.

"It's two dozen. I sent you the first one earlier, and it just didn't seem like enough. I wanted to give you more. Do you like them?" His eyes implored, pleading.

"Twenty-five yellow roses," her voice was barely a whisper. "They are perfect, Baxter."

She reached up and pulled him down so she could kiss him. The roses were crushed between them, but neither of them noticed. Baxter pulled her closer still. It was a sign. A sign that it was okay for her to move on. Eva could almost hear her mother whispering in her ear; she knew that she was holding her future in her arms. She knew as the electricity of that kiss passed between them that she didn't have to run away any more.

About the Author

Visit Mary Malcolm on the web at
www.marymalcolm.com

The Lost Highway

by

L.A. Mitchell

Dedication

For Donna, who took dictation of my seventh grade novel and knew me as a writer before I believed it myself. Love you, Sis.

Above the forgotten highway, where west Texas winds sculpted hot, liquid images against the baked asphalt, three vultures circled, emaciated and impatient. Their wings beat a clumsy rhythm, an impromptu death march punctuated by the occasional bottle-rocket cries of a nearby hawk. The three awaited the parched remains of Rye Dalton. Not yet dead in the physical sense—far from it—but in the truest sense of all that mattered.

Sweat plunged between Rye's shoulder blades, seeking escape from his overheated skin in the cotton fibers of his T-shirt. For three miles he'd pushed his scrap-heap motorcycle past outdated mile posts and hollowed-out pump stations with empty promises of fuel. At mile marker 217, four hundred miles from his destination, the Silver Spur Gas-N-Go materialized from a shifting mirage. An enormous cowboy hat, large enough to take flight in a dust devil, perched atop the sagging roofline.

Rye heaved his bike the final stretch to a mecca of shade over the pumps and thrust his foot against the rusted kickstand hard enough to break it. He sagged against the crumbling storefront. A gnat buzzed in the heat of his exhale and landed on his cheek, an unwelcome enemy snared on his flypaper skin.

He checked his watch. *Damn it.*

Muscles in his neck and shoulders hardened, roasted from pushing the two hundred pound pile of junk he should have abandoned long before his fuel line broke. Long before her exotic scent disappeared and all that remained were the memories of her straddled against his backside, racing the mistakes they longed to leave in a dust trail.

A steady hush, stronger than the wind curling through his ears, strengthened. He fished an old bus ticket from his front pocket—every number, every detail— as faded and smooth as a wish stone.

The noise, louder now, came from the direction he'd just traveled. South.

His lethargic gaze traced the dotted curves of the date stamp, and he became lost in the vast canyon between then and now until the darker memories coiled like a diamondback rattler. A sudden gust lifted the paper and carried it, leaving four quarters and a wad of lint to the mercy of the blast-furnace winds.

He scrambled after the crinkled stub, gravel puncturing the worn denim across his knees, and captured it at the base of a wild fescue. His hope of finding her again, as he once had, restored to the safety of his pocket, he realized the sound was an approaching car.

White. Almost invisible through the heat cloud had the cherry-red vinyl seats not harnessed the glaring sun. The classic, rocket-shaped convertible crawled along the fractured road. Fast enough to know the '59 Thunderbird still ran. Slow enough for him to absorb the driver within.

A woman. Thick, blond hair snaked beneath a gauzy, patterned scarf. Tied beneath her chin, its triangular point snapped in the breeze like a flag in a presidential motorcade. Jeweled, almond-shaped sunglasses concealed most of her face. Doo-wap music blared from the car's speakers.

Perfect. Fifty miles from civilization, and he was about to be rescued by Doris Day.

Rye dodged the gas pumps and broke into a run. His sweat-soaked jeans cinched his thighs like a wet blanket clinging to a drowning man.

"Hey!" He waved his arms above his head, a universal distress call masked by exhausted panic, and charged the road. "Hey, wait!"

Whitewall tires, rims mirroring the late afternoon sun, continued to eat the highway at a steady clip. The woman's face stayed centered on the road ahead, her brow creased. Her teeth, as white and straight as the path she carved through the desolate landscape, sank into a pillow of electric red lipstick.

Words from the song reached a crescendo and faded.

...just a lonely boy, lonely and blue, I'm all alone...

Rye stormed the faded yellow line at the road's center and entered a choking nest of exhaust. Four round taillights and a glistening boomerang emblem dissolved in the stifling heat.

"You blind, lady?" He raised his sleeve to his face and wiped away a fresh layer of sweat. "Christ!"

Three winged shadows eclipsed the sun, circling him in a halo as tight as chalk marks around a cadaver.

He growled at the buzzards, an animalistic release of everything that had gone wrong to this point. This road. This moment in time. He'd found the crossroads—that intangible instant where a decision comes on with such gravity, it has the power to alter the course of a lifetime— and he'd slipped a half day behind schedule. He had to make it.

Rye plucked the quarters from his palm. His boots scraped the gravel as he approached the storefront. No sign of life other than a few scavengers with exoskeletons and hairless tails. Through the window, a soda machine panel illuminated the dusky shadows.

"Bingo."

His tongue squeezed the remaining moisture from his body in anticipation. The ground yielded no forced-entry weapon to shatter the door's glass, so he trekked to his bike and retrieved his leather jacket. One punch added a B&E to his stale criminal record.

Eight ounces of sugary cola and one long overdue leak later, he'd scrounged for enough rubber tubing to MacGyver his way to the next town. He planted his sore backside on the ground beside the bike and flicked his switchblade to cut the old line.

A song, plucky and dismal, drifted into his awareness.

... in the world's come over you?...

Gravel popped a car's undercarriage. Rye squinted into the bright sun. The v-shaped chrome emblem on the convertible's passenger door lured his gaze. He wiped the fuel dripping from his fingertips against his jeans and stood.

The woman navigated the mint-condition, wing-tipped boat to a stop behind his bike, its idling engine as commanding as a battleship on a desert ocean. She turned toward him, but offered no words.

"Feelin' guilty?" he asked.

"Help me. Please."

Her words escaped in hushed tones, as if she were letting him in on some grand conspiracy. The absurdity of it all—the car, her get-up, the music—evaporated the instant he zeroed in on the way her full lower lip quivered.

He sidestepped a few inches to where the roofline blocked the sun, but her ridiculous glasses and scarf concealed most of her face. "What's wrong?"

"I've lost my way."

"Where you headed?"

"Rock Springs Gulch." She plucked her glasses from her face. A line matching the slant of the lenses divided sunburned cheeks from a tired mixture of pale skin and smeared makeup. "I must have taken a wrong turn."

"Rock Springs," he echoed, more to recover from the distraction of her appearance than to internalize her destination. He'd expected to see the wrinkled face of a baby boomer reliving her youth. Instead, his gaze navigated the flawless skin of a vibrant young woman. "Got a map?"

She blinked as if he'd asked her to hand over her purse at gunpoint, then leaned across the console to the mirrored glove box. The movement cinched her fitted yellow sundress across her full breasts—torpedo shaped, like the T.V. moms from the fifties.

Her shaking fingertips, long and unadorned, crawled through the compartment, spilling papers onto the car's immaculate red floorboard. The stagnate summer air stirred and brought with it the heady scent of flowers. Rain, maybe, to a parched land.

"No map," she confessed.

Her gaze lifted. Reluctantly. He could feel it. Every meticulous inch of how he must have looked—a vagrant, a thief, a man on the edge of hope—until her bluebonnet eyes paused, and she took in more than just his own stare. She captured his breath. Against the harsh land pressing down on them like an immovable force, the gentle curve of her eyelids and the deep blue oasis beyond made him forget. His hard luck. The broken bike. All of it.

He remembered the ticket stub in his pocket and bit the inside of his cheek to punish himself for forgetting what he'd driven all night to do.

As if bound by some ancient rule of propriety, she broke the connection first. Her gaze sought something safer. Less intense. He glanced over his shoulder, in the direction her attention had wandered, to the pay phone at the corner of the building. The receiver, strangled by a glistening metal cord, swayed like a pendulum.

"Phone's dead. Already tried it." Rye glanced up. Behind the drop-cloth haze, the sun had slipped lower on the horizon. "What's in Rock Springs, if you don't mind me askin'?"

"I'm late. I'm supposed to meet someone."

Maybe it was the way she took a sudden interest in what lay beyond him or her sweet scent; he knew without a doubt that someone was a man.

"Stay here. I'll get you a map, Ms...," he drawled expectantly.

"Eve."

Damned if she didn't have the most forbidden name to go along with the Thunderbird's apple red interior and her full, flushed lips. The breeze stirred. A blond strand escaped the scarf at her temple and curled around one of a dozen transparent yellow roses crowding the sheer fabric. Rye remembered being fourteen on a blanket in a meadow, the girl-next-door's blond hair spilled across his barely-there bicep.

He started toward the building.

"You didn't tell me your name."

Rye paused and turned. He stared at the clean, manicured fingertips she held poised in the air between them. From the back pocket of his jeans, he unhooked his greasy hand and grasped hers. "Rye Dalton."

He expected her hand to slip away, a reflex against his viscous grip, but her hold strengthened.

"You're real."

"'Scuse me?"

"Nothing. It's crazy. It's just..."

In the heavy pause, she dangled between reluctance and confession. He became convinced the heat had taken hold of her mind.

"I was hoping you were a dream—that this, was all a dream. A nightmare, really."

"Ms. Eve, I've never been anyone's dream." He glanced at the striped pink hat box in the backseat, the monogrammed initial E sandwiched between an N and W. New. "I'll get you that map."

Her soft hand slipped away. Lips, once unsteady and trembling, parted to speak, then closed as if nothing more could be said. Somewhere in Rock Springs, she'd find what she was looking for. Escape whatever nightmare had seized her. And somewhere, at a bus stop along the Atlanta to L.A. run, he'd find the woman he'd lost and make everything right again.

Inside the abandoned store, he rifled through greeting cards with gnawed edges and Texas-shaped souvenirs. His gaze stopped on a vinyl photo sleeve, packed with random snapshots of people who looked like they'd found the secret to eternal happiness. He considered swiping one, keeping the stranger's pictures because he had no more of his own, but he'd never been one to steal much of anything. The empty slots would disturb him more than never learning life's greatest secret, anyway.

Rye glanced up. Through the window's brown film, he watched the woman take a drag from a slim cigarette and pace the length of the gas pump island.

Beneath a fallen turnstile of baseball caps, Rye uncovered a state map—a paper bribe, not of money, but direction. One map, faded from years of direct sunlight, in exchange for a retro-theme park ride, complete with a melodramatic actress, to the nearest civilization.

He unfolded the crisp panels and zeroed in on the blue arteries and the vast expanse of white between towns. Different from the nervous spread dotting the eastern half of the state. Five years ago, had she felt it, too? His only love's infectious, gypsy impulses, drained away in the quiet, isolated void.

He studied the map on his way out the door, his eyes scanning for key words. "I don't see a Rock..."

Tires squealed in a wide arc against the pavement. He glanced up and saw the convertible, a white blur of tethered scarf and cherry-red seats and lips headed north. His last, best chance of making it to Dallas on time. Gone.

Rye charged his bike and slammed his boot sole

against the engine. "Son-of-a—" The rusted heap fell to the dirt, his curse swallowed in the crash of metal. Every derogatory female name fired through his mind, but none of them categorized the woman he'd just encountered. Insane, maybe, but something about her defied his usual reaction to being screwed.

Above him, the three forager's naked heads glazed orange in the waning daylight.

He righted his bike and resumed the task of splicing the hose he'd found behind the soda machine. Stars bubbled to the surface of the deepening sky. The first hint of temperate night air filled his lungs. His anger subsided, replaced with thoughts of yellow roses. Ripe lips. Torpedoes.

Fuel line secured, Rye recapped a metal gas can and stashed it beside a van on cinder blocks around back. In the twenty minutes that had passed, he'd looked up expectantly more than once, not at any one sound or instinct, but from a dismal place he couldn't understand.

He told himself he had no interest in who Eve was, what might be waiting for her in Rock Springs, or why she chose to travel this deserted highway alone, like some kind of reincarnation of a squeaky-clean era, long dead.

His only possessions secured firmly in his pack, he stared down at the faded map, fluttering beneath his front tire. He suppressed the urge to grab it. Search for Rock Springs one last time. In the map's folds, he might find evidence of smeared ink; or maybe, the town had simply fallen into the same white void, hell-bent on causing heartache to anyone who dared visit.

Rye reached into his pocket. Beside his lone ignition key lay the ticket he'd used to board a Greyhound bound for Vegas five years earlier. Instead of the fast money he needed, he'd found a familiar face, a willing spirit and a boyhood love that had never dimmed.

He mounted his bike and turned the key. One hundred and fifty horsepower shuddered beneath him, weakened from the day he'd driven it off the show room floor. Tired, maybe, from chasing something down the road that never seemed to materialize from the dream-like haze.

The throttle's black teeth sank into his slick palms.

He double-checked his makeshift hose, focused on the glowing line where earth met sky, and laid a thin trail of fresh rubber at mile marker 217, determined to steal back every stretch of ground he'd lost.

Rye's yellow headlamp snared a bright object a quarter of a mile away.

White.

Before he could make out the red-orbed taillights floating in the darkness or the chrome-tipped fins anchoring the bull's eye spare tire case, he saw her.

Old fashioned white shoes, pumped to a modest height, stirred against the black pavement. He savored every inch of her shapely calves, the breeze kicking the knee-length hemline of her sundress to a disappointing elevation. The word on her hatbox came to mind. New. Her legs were definitely a new development, a distraction from his encroaching guilt.

He didn't want to stop. Couldn't stop. He'd traveled the desperate, bizarre detour with her already. Pride straightened his posture in the seat. She'd given him the polite, 50's version of the middle finger when she'd abandoned him at the station. The present-day's version itched to be released in his seventy mile per hour wake as it rearranged her matronly wardrobe. Torpedo, baby.

But the heavens conspired, pressing the night into his consciousness. The void encroached and became the third traveler on the lost highway in a battle of wills. He caught Eve's movement, a hand swiping her cheek, as she leaned against the driver's side door, scarf gone. His grip eased on the throttle.

What if his bike wouldn't start again?

His eyelids slid closed. The engine vibrated the seat between his thighs. A sickening feeling stirred through every pulsing muscle. Vertigo, maybe. Shadowy thoughts raced to the next possible traveler. What if he were a psychopath with a preoccupation for gutting women?

The thunder beneath Rye subsided as he opened his eyes. Admitted defeat in a standoff with a crying woman. Five minutes, tops. Then, he'd go.

Close enough now to see the tension fade from her face, her lips spread to an almost-smile, Rye edged his bike from the blacktop and rolled to a stop behind the convertible. His headlamp's lone eye illuminated her black and white license plate. Texas. 1960. An original—like the ones hanging over the smoke pit of every barbecue dive south of the Red River.

Odd, how every detail fit into her carefully-crafted display.

He reached for the ignition key, his fingers poised on its wide base while he reconsidered killing the engine. Then she was before him, her faded red lips moving with the rhythm of her body, her words buried beneath the bike's growl. Hearing her voice, the melody of its subtle, innocent rise, became a temptation he could no longer resist. He turned the key.

The motor stuttered and silenced, snuffed out by a chorus of night creatures crowding the brush. Filling the white void.

"I'm never going to get there." No anger. Just a statement. Detached. Relieved, maybe.

"You took off."

"I told you, I'm late. The day's almost over."

"Won't they come looking for you?"

"Who?"

"Whoever you're supposed to meet."

Eve turned and retreated, closer to the Thunderbird, as if its dashboard glow and hypnotic music housed a slow, magnetic pull. Somehow, he couldn't picture her without the car.

"We've never seen each other. If I don't find my way to the covered bridge at Rock Springs, it'll all be for nothing." She glanced down. Her fingers threaded and tightened into a white-knuckled fist. "I could look like a million other girls."

"Not around here."

Eve glanced over her shoulder. One golden curl teased her collar. Never quite making eye contact, she looked like a World War II pin-up girl tossing well-wishes to troops ready to charge into combat. Her smooth cheeks flushed red, not from any sunburn or the haunting glow of taillights, but as a direct result of what she must have believed was a compliment.

His heart lightened, relieved she never had to know

137

what he'd meant. A freak.

He climbed from the seat. Blood surged through his rigid muscles. "It's late. You should find a safe place for the night."

"I have to find it before midnight." She smacked her ankle, then scraped her nails along the silky nylons covering her calves. A nearby cricket's shrill protest grew louder.

"That town you're looking for? Must have the name wrong. Rock Springs doesn't exist on the map."

"That's impossible. My father spoke of it many times."

"Where're you from?"

"The coast. Near Galveston."

"Why drive all this way for someone you've never met?"

She glanced up the road, the direction she'd headed before something—some truth or fear—had stopped her, but offered nothing.

"You're right. It's not my business." He raised his hands in surrender. "None of this is."

"You'll think it's strange."

No more than a flighty woman living in a past not her own.

"You may laugh."

Rye approached the car's left fin and gave into the temptation to run his palm along its sleek length. "Try me."

"It's a pact, really. Between friends. On graduation night, we found a box of photographs in the attic that belonged to my father. He was a traveling salesman—household cleaners. He took pictures at every stop to prove he was a trustworthy employee."

Eve leaned against the car beside him, close enough to stir the air near his arm. Rye tried to remember the name of the white blossom that bloomed at night.

"We each drew a snapshot from the box and made a declaration. If we hadn't found true love in exactly one year—to the day—we'd go to the place in our photo. Right there, waiting for us, we'd find it."

An energy permeated her from within. A contagious optimism so alien to him, so hard to pull off, it had to be genuine.

"A childish game, really."

"And yet, you're here." Rye shifted and slid his hands into his front pockets. The ticket stub settled near his right thumb. He withdrew his hand.

"So I am." Her gaze skittered to the security of the crescent moon. "What do you know about true love, Mr. Dalton?"

"Enough to know you won't find it at the end of this godforsaken stretch of land or any other. No matter how close you come, it always outdistances you."

"How very cynical. You must have had your heart broken by someone you loved very much."

He didn't know what to say. How had his humanitarian gesture ended up on ground too raw to explore? He cleared his throat and muttered, "Still have the photo?"

"Yes," she whispered, but her gaze lingered on his face, his lips, as if the abrupt shift in topic had left her behind.

A smile slipped past his resolve to remain disconnected. "Can I see it?"

"Oh." She turned and plucked a curved photo sandwiched between the parking brake and the dashboard's chrome lining. The white undergarment that caused her skirt to balloon out slipped into view. Her heel rose from the pavement. Very Doris Day. "Here it is."

She presented the snapshot, a touchstone of hope he dared not crush, and moved closer, bringing with her the unmistakable pull of the night, the soft crooning of a man's voice from the radio and the intoxicating nearness of a beautiful, genuine spirit.

For a moment, he stared at the photo in the light of his bike's headlamp, unable to see anything but the sway of her pearl-drop earring. The contemplative turn of her head as she studied its subject matter.

"Do you see..." Her enthusiastic words stalled in the realization that he studied her instead. "... anything?"

He recovered a breath too late. The disturbing tide of guilt returned—not for considering leaving her behind, but for forgetting what lay ahead. Hours ago, he'd thought of nothing but his gypsy love on a west-bound trip. Now, the girl—barely a woman—whose shoulder brushed his own, who'd materialized in the shifting mirage of empty space in the unforgiving west Texas landscape, left him craving more.

His mind absorbed the photo's image. Red cedar lay in generous planks, vaulted against the stark background. Live oaks twisted in the purple and orange layers of a heat-charged sunset on the plains. On the photo's padded white border, someone had written *Rock Springs Gulch— 1951.*

The D.J.'s voice broke into his thoughts. "Here's a brand new track from Elvis Presley. Enjoy."

The song's pulsing, Latin rhythm lifted into the star-filled night.

...It's now or never. Come hold me tight...

A knot formed in Rye's stomach, the disconnectedness between rational and crazy as disarming as her fragrance. "Impossible."

"What's impossible?" Eve asked.

Rye stared at the radio, its red needle severing the otherworldly glow at a number near one hundred. He remembered four white crosses beside the road, decayed with time. He pictured flames rising from the red slats. The death of a small town in the aftermath of a tragedy. His stomach churned at the memory of staring out the back of his family's station wagon at the charred remains of a bridge at the base of a creek bed.

"Do you know this place?"

"I've heard of it. It's a legend in this area."

"Really?" Eve's face bloomed in a spectacular display of perfect teeth and glistening eyes.

... My heart was captured, my soul surrendered...

The hot, liquid sculpture took shape. Her old-fashioned mannerisms, her reserved innocence, her optimism, blended into the picture of a woman who'd set off in search of love and become lost along the way.

Just as he had.

Rye dismissed the ridiculous notion that the Thunderbird somehow carried her to a destination not of her own time, but of his.

"Out on Highway 71." He'd been what, ten, when he'd seen the road closed sign? The painful clutch in his gut eased when he realized she couldn't have been one of the four victims.

"Can you give me directions?"

"Be hard to find now."

She bounded close and slipped her delicate hand around his. A simple, unguarded gesture that weakened his knees. "Will you take me there?" she whispered.

... For who knows when, we'll meet again this way...

Rye stepped back, summoning images of a blanket in a meadow. Arms wrapped around his leather jacket, the vibration of the bike the only force strong enough to slip between him and the woman he'd loved.

"Turnoff's down the road, 'bout thirty miles. Can't miss it."

Eve's long, dark eyelashes lowered to rest upon her apple-red cheeks. An exhale, warm and smoky, brushed his neck and entered the night slowly. Unsteady. Her hand slipped away. "All right."

Gravel crunched beneath her white heels. She opened the convertible's massive door and slipped into the seat, blond curls cascading down her back. As perfect there as she'd ever been.

A sense of finality swept over him, as acute as the loss of her touch against his skin. Somehow he knew the snapshot of her driving away would be his last glimpse. Another regret to fill the void.

...Tomorrow will be too late. It's now or never...

Eve turned the ignition. The engine's deep revolutions overpowered the night.

The harder Rye tried to reconstruct his memories into a living, breathing conviction that he was doing the right thing, the more they scattered like dried wheat. A wish he could never get back.

She wrapped her hand around the gearshift and tugged.

"Wait," Rye shouted.

Red taillights glared against his faded jeans. The convertible's front end nosed down.

He circled the car, closer now to the passenger's side.

"When, exactly, was your graduation?"

"Why, last year." Eve's perfectly-shaped brows distorted. "Weren't you listening?"

Rye battled what felt like a sagebrush lodged in his throat. "1959?"

"Yes," she said, as if it were the most obvious answer in the world.

He thought of a handful of ways to tell her the photograph was more than fifty years old. That she'd driven, not to the destination of some childish game, but to an unexplainable place far beyond what she had bargained for. The memory of her quivering lip returned. Her fear, and his capacity to make her forget. All of it.

Rye wrapped his heated palm around the cool, chrome door handle.

He glanced at his bike. Corroded. Broken. He slipped his other hand into his pocket, the inertia of what he'd wanted for so long and the worn softness of the ticket stub conspiring to sway his decision. The gravity of his choice weighted his tired feet like shackles connecting his boots.

Two roads converged on a lost highway. One, the same tired road of self-doubt he'd traveled each day since love had left him behind. The other, an unknown filled with possibilities. Neither a guarantee of eternal happiness.

The wind shifted and brought with it the scent of night flowers. Rain. New horizons. And he knew he needed to believe in something as much as the unforgettable woman before him.

"I'll take you."

He opened the door and sank into the smooth vinyl, as supple as a woman's skin. A quick pinch of his watch buttons illuminated the readout.

11:40.

"How long will it take to get there?" she asked, the same captivated stare he'd witnessed earlier fixed on his timepiece.

"Twenty minutes, if you floor it."

Eve's face, illuminated as much from within as from the moonlight spilling down over the canopy of night, softened, her hope-filled smile an answer to his own.

At mile marker 190, where the wind snatched away his faded ticket, a sacrifice to the void that had brought them together, the '59 Thunderbird joined the highway headed south.

The Lost Highway

"Lonely Boy." Songwriters Paul Anka and Joe Dowell. Recorded by Paul Anka (1959)

"What in the World's Come Over You." Songwriter Giovanni Scafone Jr. Recorded by Jack Scott (1960)

"It's Now or Never." Songwriters Aaron Schroeder and Wally Gold. Recorded by Elvis Presley (1960)

About the Author

L.A. Mitchell has called Texas home three distinct times in her life. A former English teacher and graduate of Texas A&M University, she now resides near Fort Worth. Her award-winning stories encompass her fascination with time theory, conspiracies and the quest for a happily ever after in dimensions that can sometimes seem worlds apart. Visit her on the web at www.la-mitchell.com.

Shotgun Seduction

by

Angi Morgan

Dedication

To my dad. A man who always had grease under his nails, kept all my cars running and loved my mother from the moment he set eyes on her.

What were the odds of walking off a plane in Dallas and seeing the one person you never wanted to see again?

Jacqueline Summer O'Connor.

The sight of her made the hair on the back of Sean Davis' neck stand up, among other parts of his anatomy. Didn't matter that he had as much in common with her as he did the Queen of England.

He was a grease monkey, spending every day of his life working on ordinary cars. She drove a Jag.

He slept in a one-room apartment on a secondhand couch where his feet dangled off the end. She lived in a thirty-room mansion.

When she kissed him, none of that had mattered. His toes had curled inside his steel-plated work boots. Her Italian high heels had dropped from her delicate feet to the sidewalk while she tangled her fingers in his hair and pressed her body to his so tightly he could barely expand his chest to breathe.

But it would never work.

She was rich. What else could he say?

"Sean?"

Damn, she'd spotted him.

He intended to keep walking, but his feet seemed to have a mind of their own and stopped him in his tracks. Unfortunately, his tracks were directly in front of the revolving door. His lack of motion forced one man to circle through again.

In the time it took her to advance the four steps separating them, he soaked up her presence like a dry sponge. The color of her hair was still an unusual blend of red and brown—redder now since she was backlit by the afternoon sun streaming through the airport windows.

The details reserved for his sleepless nights flooded his system, making his blood burn. She looked gorgeous. Every towering inch of her. The bright, sleeveless dress emphasized each curve he tortured himself to forget.

"Can't talk now, Jacqui, I've gotta run. My company's

sending a car." He moved toward the exit, away from his annoyed fellow passengers.

"You're meeting me, Sean. Didn't anyone tell you?"

No. No. And no. His feet, acting on their own again, came to a screeching halt. There had to be someone else there. But no one in the crowded airport held up a sign with his name. No one else was waiting. Just his luck.

"Do you have any luggage?" she asked as if nothing had happened between them. As if they were nothing more than two friends at an arranged meeting.

"I'm traveling light. They said the clothes would be provided." He patted his duffle draped over his shoulder, trying to maintain the same cool she sustained. "Why are *you* here?"

"My car's parked just outside." She steered him toward the exit ignoring his question.

"Wait a minute." Several heads turned to look at them and Sean took her elbow, guiding her to the side of the crowd. He lowered his voice, "What's going on?"

Touching her, even with a hundred people watching, brought everything from last year back to the surface. His decision to end their relationship attacked his conscience like metal shavings in an engine. Combustion began when he met her fiery amber eyes. Connecting with her skin, his fingers made it as far as her forearm—just as soft as his dreams remembered. He yanked back his hand.

Avoid physical contact at all costs.

Too bad it wasn't winter when every part of her body would have been covered by a coat. Every part of her body *should* be covered, so normal men could function without major damage to their brains.

"I was hired by Atlantis Photography for a magazine spread." He stepped further away and she followed. "Mark Bertram specifically said I'd be met by the head honcho."

Either the slight arch of her well-shaped brow or the fact she didn't argue brought him to a crashing halt. You didn't have to hit him over the head twice.

"You own Atlantis Photography?"

"More or less."

"Which one? More or less?"

"Well, I wouldn't call me the head honcho." Her face

lit up with teasing laughter one second, then his lungs deflated and didn't fill back up during the next..

Too close. She was too close for him to think. He placed his hands on her hips with every intention of setting her back a couple of feet.

Instead, his hands slid up her back as she snuggled closer. She fanned her fingers through his hair, pushing it back past his temple. Even a dense guy like him recognized when teasing stopped and anticipation began.

"I missed you, Sean," she whispered.

A buzzing in his ears replaced all logical thought when her eyes closed, preparing for his kiss.

Jacqui's moist lips settled against his and he couldn't pull away. He didn't want to pull away. She tasted like vanilla cola and smelled better than fresh chocolate chip cookies.

God, he was starved for her. Her body melted into his aching hardness like ice in the desert.

Whoa. Remember that failed attempt at mixing the classes? He couldn't afford for her father to maneuver things so he lost his modeling career. He had too much riding on the money from this shoot. The garage loan, Stefani's tuition.... With a groan he broke the kiss while Jacqui blinked her long lashes up at him.

"We are not going down this road again." He couldn't afford her, emotionally or financially. Sean stepped away too fast and ended up tumbling backwards.

****

If Sean's hands hadn't been stretched toward the ceiling as if someone had a gun pointed at him, he might have been able to save himself. It happened so fast Jacqui couldn't prevent him falling over two suitcases, a bag of souvenirs, and a dozen welcome-home yellow roses.

After turning red with humiliation and storming through the exit door, Sean hadn't said a word to her during the two-hour drive. The radio had covered the silence, but now they were close to the ranch and far from the car tuner's capability. She wouldn't aid Sean's silence by playing any CDs.

"Are you certain you're okay?"

He didn't budge, just sat there with an unopened soda can warming between his hand and the back of his

150

skull. Poor thing. His head must hurt—and she really hadn't meant to laugh—but sorting him out from all the luggage had been just too funny.

She'd planned for the time driving to the ranch to be filled with conversation. Time to discover if he'd missed her as much as she'd missed him.

She wanted to explain why she'd asked for him specifically for this shoot. They deserved a chance to find out if something more could develop in their relationship. Once they arrived he'd be on a roller coaster of fittings, makeup, and work. There wouldn't be time for talking.

If only her father hadn't interfered last year, she would know the answers already. She'd also know whether her feelings were real or not. Why had he just stopped everything last year?

Money. That's what his sister had told her when Sean wouldn't return her calls. Well then, she'd just have to prove to him that money didn't matter. Especially having money.

If only.... The small silver spurs her mother had given to her as a child jingled from the mirror where they always hung, a constant reminder of the wonderful woman who had been taken at such a young age. She could still hear her mother's favorite mantra: "'If onlys' are fixable regrets."

Jacqui had three days to prove she was just a normal woman. She had three days to make certain there weren't any regrets. Life was too short to leave any possibility unanswered.

He looked as good as she remembered. Gorgeous sandy blond hair and a perfect body that seemed even more fit than last year. Chiseled features, the square jaw any western ad campaign longed for, and perfect blue eyes that made women swoon. She'd experienced that herself. Except...well, there was a sadness there. Or was it just the headache?

"Please hear me out, Sean. I know what my father did last year," she said while turning off the highway and risked a long glance at his rugged profile. "He was completely wrong, but you're being just as stubborn."

"Stubborn?" The can dropped to his lap. "I'm being stubborn?"

"Yes, and childish by not talking to me."

"Your father hired thugs to 'warn' me to stay away from you. I lost my apartment and my father's garage because your father bought the loan. My sister had to go to work to stay in school. I think I have a damn good reason not to talk to you."

"Whether you want anything to do with me or not, Sean, you can at least let me make it up to Stefani."

"We don't want your charity," he said with a cynical tone she'd never heard from him before.

"It's repayment."

"Is this a mercy assignment? Did they really want me or did you tell them to hire me? Does your father know I'm on my way to his home? And why is the shoot at your ranch anyway?"

"The designer is a friend of mine" Georgette had jumped on Sean's picture, mouth salivating in anticipation of getting to run her hands over his abs. "My firm is handling the promotion for her line of western wear. It's what I do."

"How could I forget?" He turned back toward the window.

There was nothing to see out there. Just miles and miles of nothing. She should know. She'd spent almost her entire life growing up outside of Jacksboro, Texas. Most of the miles currently around them belonged to her overprotective father.

It didn't matter that she was twenty-seven years old. Until three months ago, his bodyguards had followed her everywhere. That is, until she'd found out about Sean losing his job.

"I skim the Internet looking for just the right model to represent the right company. I came across a man in a tux promoting a charity auction for children. I flew to Atlanta specifically for the event, certain this man—yes, you—couldn't be as real as his photos indicated. Real, Sean. A real person who cared."

At least he'd turned away from the window and was looking at her now. Gawking, but toward her instead of the Texas brush. Geez, being this forthright actually made her throat hurt.

"Breaking up..." She couldn't swallow, couldn't get

enough spit in her mouth to talk. *Finish, dang it!* This was it. Forget the humiliation and horrible rejection she'd wallowed in for half a year. "I brought you out here to see if there was a chance we could work things out. I didn't find out Dad interfered until three months ago. I actually thought you'd had your little fling and that you were done."

"You couldn't pick up the phone and call? You had to haul me out here to Nowheresville, Texas?"

"Atlantis Photo wanted the shoot on a working ranch." *And after Stefi told me about the money problems, I wanted you to see the real me. But I'll keep that tidbit to myself for now.* "So you took up modeling full time?"

His low growl was probably a bad sign. She shouldn't have brought up the subject of work. Although, from what she'd found out, he was doing fairly well with local modeling jobs in Atlanta. He loved being an auto mechanic and her father had taken his family business away from him. Bought it right out from under him, through manipulating loan companies.

"I didn't have much choice. After the charity auction, some offers came in from local vendors.." He laughed under his breath. "I kind of needed the money."

"I am so sorry about that."

He was looking around, out the front window, out the side window. Tapping the fingers of one hand on the dash. Curling his fingers around the soda can with the other How could she keep a conversation going with someone who just didn't want to talk to her?

"We'll be there in a few minutes."

"Great." He took a deep breath and exhaled slowly. It was the only noise in the BMW besides the echo of gravel hitting the undercarriage. "I like my life the way it is, Ms. O'Conner. You have your answer about working things out. It's no."

****

"Everything going okay?"

Sean heard Jacqui's voice everywhere. It didn't matter if she was working horses in the field, feeding chickens, or raking muck in the corral. He still heard the sensual soft Texas inflection he found adorable and that caused him to lose his concentration.

153

He managed to avoid her most of the time, but he couldn't get her out of his head. Hell, why should the past two days be any different from the last twelve months? Her daddy could still weigh in with the money thing and demand Atlantis hire someone else for the national campaign. He'd lose the money and a chance to get back to the life he knew. That new garage wouldn't be for sale forever.

This shoot had turned into a great opportunity and would cinch the garage loan. The photographer liked him and they worked well together. His agent had already called, confirming more shoots that would pay for Stefi's fall tuition. A national campaign wasn't anything he could turn down. Modeling wasn't his first choice for a career, but it sure paid a helluva lot more than getting grease under his nails.

"Hey, Sean, you still with us?" J.D. snapped his fingers while handing the camera off to his assistant. "We need to reload and relocate. Jacqui has arranged for a campfire back over some ridge to show off the jean jacket. Ooo, I feel so cowboyish. See ya' in a couple of hours."

"This is it, lovey," Georgette Watley, the over-sexed designer, said. "Last set of clothes should be hanging in the bunkhouse. God, I'm sooo glad Jacqui found you."

She stroked his shoulders, smoothing the open shirt they'd been featuring. He was getting used to the fawning. Sort of.

"You are exactly what I had in mind for this western line. Every last rippling muscle of you."

Plastering a tight-lipped smile to his face, he shook his head. What could he say? Thank you would come later. It was a job. Right?

Jacqui's friends, Jacqui's crew, Jacqui's house, Jacqui's everything. Whatever he said would get right back to her and he just wasn't ready for that. Not yet.

Back at the bunkhouse there was little peace. The small photo crew was all housed there, along with several ranch hands. He still had a few hours before he needed to be anywhere, so he changed into some grease-stained jeans from home and decided to look around. If only he could find a car that needed work. But he couldn't afford to mess up his hands. Damn.

"Just wandering?" Jacqui's voice was just behind him this time. She fell into step with him, her hands linked behind her back.

"You did say you wanted me to see where you lived."

"Surprised?"

There was a twinkle in her eyes as if she knew he had assumed the house was huge. It had only four bedrooms, not thirty. This was a working cattle ranch. Everything was moderate. Nicely kept-up and not run-down. It didn't ooze filthy rich although he knew she was.

"I have something for you." She pushed a straw hat into his hands.

"Uh, I really can't accept—"

"Sure you can. Dad sent it out. Wanna see the house?"

Wearing the western cowboy boots given to him for the photo shoot, he squeezed the hat on his head and *Urban Cowboy* popped into his mind. He pulled the hat back off and hurried to catch up with an excited Jacqui, who was talking ninety miles a minute, but he really couldn't hear what she said. His eyes scanned the house watching for the man who had made him so aware of the importance of money.

Did he really want to go in there? Daddy was home. When he'd arrived this morning, he'd made it very loudly known that he wasn't to be bothered. It was obvious Jacqui hadn't asked his permission before scheduling the photo op. The huge man—who anyone would automatically call "the Duke" because he looked like John Wayne in his sixties—was barely pacified when Jacqui told him the ranch would receive some publicity.

As the girl in his nightly dreams leapt up the three steps to the veranda-style porch, Sean was no longer afraid of or furious with John O'Conner. He had lots of reasons to punch the man's lights out, but the emotion just wasn't there. When his foot hit the third step, he hesitated. Jacqui paused with the screen open and quieted. He hated that look of disappointment, especially from her. He wanted her to smile again.

But all he could do was gulp, trying to swallow the knot lodged in his throat. He couldn't see, think, or feel anything but Jacqui. He cared too much about her to hurt her father. He wouldn't do it, no matter how much he longed to tell the man where to get off.

"I don't really have anything to say to him, Jacqui." And couldn't say anything to her. They didn't belong on the same side of anything and it was a damn shame. He side-tossed the hat like a Frisbee into her hands. "Sorry, it doesn't...fit."

Jacqui watched him lope away until he reached the corral. She needed to help Jessie anyway. With all the extra mouths to feed, she'd never hear the end of it if she didn't lend a hand in the kitchen.

"I didn't peg him for a coward," her dad stated from the bottom of the stairs, grabbing the hat she'd placed on the rail.

"How dare you call him that after what you did? He's a better man than you'll ever think yourself to be. He's practically raised his younger sister and even after you stole his garage and threatened him with your goons— don't try to deny it. He's still managed to send Stefani to college, putting every penny he has aside for her."

"He didn't make it up the steps. Either he's a coward, or he doesn't love you very much."

Well that's what I set all this up to find out. If she moved out and took the Duke out of the picture? Would she be able to find out then?

"I don't know why I even try talking to you" She turned toward the kitchen, but a knock on the door made her stop while her dad answered.

"Mr. O'Conner, I thought it was time we actually met. I'm Sean Davis. I believe you bought my garage in Atlanta last year."

The big man everyone was afraid of had nothing to say. He ignored the outstretched hand before him and shook his head. He hadn't even opened the screen door.

"Sorry I don't have time for a long-overdue man-to-man talk, but J.D. decided he wants some more pictures. Nice to have met you. Oh, and I'll be needing that hat after all."

Her father stuttered a goodbye as Sean pulled the door open, winked at Jacqui, retrieved the hat, and placed it on his head. He actually whistled, then leapt off the porch, not bothering with the steps.

Not a coward, but maybe just a bit slow on the uptake. Maybe Sean just needed a little reminding how well he got along with her.

"You might as well learn to like the guy, Dad. He's the one I'm going to marry."

Running from the room before her father could recover his breath from the choking-coughing fit, Jacqui headed off to help Jessie with the rest of the barbeque preparations. Twenty-five racks of ribs had been in the smoker since yesterday, courtesy of an unknowing John O'Conner. It was the least he could do. She took the potatoes off the stove to drain for a traditional potato salad—something she could do without Jessie's supervision.

The campfire was not only the last shoot, it was the farewell party. She had honestly thought she'd be able to have more than three words with Sean before he left for Atlanta tomorrow. Oh my, the look on her father's face. Both when Sean was at the door and when she'd said she'd marry him.

Goodness knew the words felt right. No scratchiness in her throat, no hesitation. She loved Sean Davis and wanted a chance at the real thing.

Now, how to make *him* realize that? They could spend more time together. Work together. After all, Georgette was practically in love with Sean too. Different reasons, of course. Georgette was just after his body.

Jacqui wanted the entire package.

Everything. Even the grease under his fingernails that she'd help him scrub many times before a date.

"And what's that mystical smile on your face for?" Jessie asked, coming back into the kitchen.

"Just thinking."

"You've been thinking like that a lot in the last couple of days."

"More like the last year," she said under her breath, but it was apparent by Jessie's laugh that she'd heard her.

"You going to do somethin' about it?" By her smile it was more than evident her father's housekeeper had a strong suspicion the reason was Sean.

"Yes. I believe I will." But why wait for more work?

Couldn't they come to some kind of decision before he left? If he left at all?

"We could always have a shotgun wedding," Jessie teased.

"Oh, Jessie, you're incorrigible." Maybe not a shotgun wedding, but what about a shotgun seduction? Now that wasn't such a bad idea.

****

The campfire burned low. The last pot had been stowed and the last ranch hand was heading back to the bunkhouse. So it surprised her to see Sean sitting on a log, staring at the fading embers.

Executing her plan was going to be easier than she'd hoped.

Her plan? That would be Plan C since plans A and B had tanked. Yeah, this was her last shot. She'd spent too many nights thinking about Mr. Right to not recognize him last year. Their magic let her know instantly Sean was the guy for her. All they needed was to talk and trust their instincts. If he could listen to her for ten minutes, she could make him understand that she was a working girl, not a spoiled princess.

And if he wouldn't sit and talk with her...? Well, Plan C waited twenty feet away.

"I thought you'd be one of the first ones to hit the hay tonight. You're leaving with J.D. and he has one of the earliest flights." She dared to sit a hair's breath away from him. He didn't move.

"Just enjoying the fire. I don't get anything like this at home."

"Last ride is heading back." She gave him a chance to leave. Or was it her point of no return? "Unless you want to ride with me."

"I don't mind the walk."

Great. Nothing around except cattle for ten or fifteen miles and he preferred to walk back to the bunkhouse instead of a short ride with her. Sean stood and stretched. The only glow came from the dying embers.

"God, there are a lot of stars." Sean had his neck craned back to look at the sky. "I don't think I've seen this many since I was at Boy Scout Camp back in junior high." He kicked at a dirt clod, then turned his eyes back toward the brilliant points of light. "I should probably be heading back." He tilted his head toward the road and waited while she caught up with him, walking with her to the old field truck.

Now or never. "Sean..." She reached inside the cab.

"Yeah?"

"Maybe you should stay a while instead of catching that flight in the morning?"

"I'm not sure that's such a great idea—" He stopped short when he saw the shotgun in her hands. "I don't think that is either. Is it loaded?"

"I needed some extra leverage to persuade you to stay. Put your hands down, Sean. It's not a hold up. Just a small detainment."

"You can't be serious." He shoved his hands into his pockets and took off down the road.

****

Staying away from Jacqui, not calling or knowing what had really happened had been the hardest thing Sean had ever done. Only one thing had kept him from following her to Texas...Stefi. But his sister had proven that she could take care of herself this past year. Not even a lack of money had kept her from continuing her education and achieving her dream.

And what about his dream? It wasn't a new garage or money. It was Jacqui. Working things out and not walking away. *That* was what he dreamed about.

"So why the hell am I walking instead of sitting under the stars like she asked?"

There was a whosh through the air and then a yank. A rope or should he say, lasso, hugged his chest, anchoring his arms to his sides. With his hands shoved in his pockets, he couldn't wiggle loose.

"All right, Jacqui. I'll stay up all night if you want me to. Just make sure I catch my plane on time. Now get this thing off me."

She gently hauled him back to her and the truck, letting the rope pool at her feet.

"Ow!" The rope pulled his skin tight, causing a slight burning sensation. "Dammit, Jacqui, take it easy."

Laughter. Yeah, she could laugh right up until the rope came off.

"I'm not certain I trust you not to leave. Am I going to have to hog tie you too?"

Not waiting for an answer, Jacqui kissed him. And he kissed her back. Kissed her like he wanted her clothes off. And he did. Daddy be damned. They'd work it out or he could forget ever seeing his grandchildren.

He wanted to hold her closer, but he couldn't push the rope from around his elbows. She traced the lines on his shirt with her fingers, slowly pushing each button through its hole. Reaching his collar, she trailed her nail across his skin and around his ear.

"Dammit, Jacqui, what are you doing?"

"Having my way with you. Go ahead and yell, Sean. I like it when your voice gets all husky."

"Yell? I've wasted too many nights trying to sleep when you invaded my dreams. Being near you is pure torture. Absolute terrorizing torture. I don't want to waste time yelling."

The thought of Jacqui back in his arms made his jeans tight, while the pit in his stomach turned into an abyss—an aching bottomless feeling that wouldn't go away anytime soon.

"Think we can get rid of the rope now?"

"I don't know," she said, smiling at him as if she wanted to eat him alive. "Can you behave yourself?"

He gulped. No other word for it. Shoot, what was he thinking? He couldn't behave with that wanton look in her eyes.

"Seriously, Sean. Do you want to talk?" She released the loop and took the rope from his body. "If you think this decision was easy..."

"The shotgun or the lasso?"

Her head snapped up and her eyes met his with that sexy inviting smile. The abyss was back and he was free-falling into it. God, when she looked at him like she wanted everything.... How would he live without her again?

He grimaced at the pain shooting through his heart. Pain that had nothing to do with bouncing on a horse all afternoon either. In the last year he hadn't looked at another woman, and he'd seen quite a few on the modeling shoots. All had been more than willing...he just wasn't able.

Coming face-to-face with Jacqui three days ago had confirmed what Stefi had preached at him all year. He was hung up on this firebrand sitting in front of him with a shotgun leaning next to her.

"I can't just sit here." He stood suddenly trying to stretch his seizing over-worked muscles.

"The keys are in the truck if you don't want to stay."

"Giving up already? I have a catch in my back. I rode a dang horse all afternoon for those extra shots J.D. wanted. You're the cowgirl, honey. I can't believe you do this every day."

"Take your shirt off. I'll grab a blanket. I might just be able to work that kink out."

Getting her hands on him was worth every minute on that stupid horse..

"You'll be more comfortable if you take those pinching boots off. I've noticed how you kind of walk like your feet hurt."

He did as ordered, tossing the boots to the other side of the log. He lay face down and she straddled his backside.

Damn, I hope she doesn't want me to talk. His voice would crack like a teenager. She put her cool hands on his hot skin and he nearly tossed her off. Had he thought torture? This had to be worse.

"Relax and just listen."

"Not a problem." Yeah, right, relax. Wasn't going to happen.

"I could waste our time explaining how protective my father is and the outrage I went through when I discovered he'd been following me last year. Naïve of me, but I really didn't know before our picture appeared in the paper."

Each fist into his flesh made him want a different kind of touch. *Concentrate.* If there was any chance of things working out, he had to let her talk.

"I know you have a problem with my money. Unfortunately, you're going to have to live with it. And baby, you better get used to it fast, because you're about to have your own."

"Huh?"

"You did a great job this week. Georgette's contacting your agent. Once these ads hit the mass market, it's just a matter of time before your new career takes off. Then you'll have enough money for everything and your body will be plastered all over magazines and billboards.."

She dug into his shoulders as if she didn't like the idea. It didn't appeal to him much either. Jacqui beat on his spine a little and another *ugh* escaped. "Wait a minute. Did you say I needed to live with your money?"

"I'd love to make a grand gesture to prove how much I love you, but I happen to like what I do, and I get paid well for it."

"Jacqui?" She pushed her fist into his shoulder blade. "Did you just say you loved me?"

All movement ceased. Then she slid to his right. He rolled to his left She meant it. The look on her face proved it. Concern. Confusion.

"I wanted to give you time last year and now. It's just...I didn't want to wait for you to realize you couldn't live without me. I needed to jump-start things and get you to listen to me."

"It's extremely hard being around you for two minutes without remembering how different we are. But I'll deal with it."

"Good. Since you really don't have a choice," she said, eyes sparkling in the firelight.

"Talking is overrated." He held his hand out to her. She laid her delicate fingers across his palm and he forced himself not to pull and yank her down to his side. Her nails skimmed up his arm to his shoulder and then across his chest. Her body followed.

Their lips met. A feeling of coming home. Of rightness. The abyss was gone. The way she fit in his arms. Fit him.

They could stay here until dawn broke over the horizon. No doubt she'd be there to make his dreams reality.

"I'm sorry," he said.

"For what?" she asked, her face flushed with desire. Desire for him.

"Sorry for giving up last year."

Another kiss and she took a deep breath. "So am I."

He eyed the shotgun leaning against the log and potential problems they faced jumped into his head. But facing the world could wait. Knowing that Jacqui loved him, he could face fifty Dukes and an army of his goons. "A rope and a shotgun—funny choice for a seduction."

"Just used my cowhand tools."

"They worked." He didn't want her away from him again.

"Good. I didn't really have a Plan D. This was my last shot." Her lips summoned him.

"I love you, Jacqueline Summer O'Connor."

"That's good to know, Sean Davis. Cause you're mine. All mine."

About the Author

Introduced to novels by her grandmother, Angi has been reading and thinking romance since falling in love with "Happily Ever Afters." At her high school reunion, no one was surprised to hear that she was writing full time. Writing is a passion she never wants to outgrow.

Angi lives in North Texas with her fairy tale husband—trying to live out their own Happily Ever After. She can be reached at Angi@angimorgan.com or through her website: www.AngiMorgan.com

My Love Dropped in at the *Drop Your Doggie Inn*

by

Gina Lee Nelson

Gina Lee Nelson

Dedication

To my husband Phil and my sons: James, Seth, and Pierce—the men in my life who give it such a delightful, robust flavor.

If, indeed, we must chew our food twenty-five times in order to digest it without mishap, there is going to be one long, extended colon in my future. I don't have the time to sit and chew my food beyond recognition.

Things have changed.

We should all take a lesson from our canine friends who don't pound their kibble into so much mush. If ever there were creatures that enjoyed their vittles, it would be dogs

But I'm not a dog, unfortunately. I'm a dentist.

In my humble opinion, teeth shouldn't be over utilized. They should be under-utilized. Unless of course, someone chooses to chew on only one side of their mouth. And that, in no shape, size, or fashion, can be considered a good thing to do. I had a stellar crossbite as a kid, which meant I always had to chew on one side of my mouth, so take my word for it.

My mother, who was as close to perfect as a mother can be, claimed the principle of twenty-five chews came from Dr. Tompkins at the Silver Spur Medical Center. Now, I'd really like to tell you what I think about the Silver Spur and that quack Dr. Tompkins. But I'm not ready to tell that story just yet.

Earlier, I said I was a dentist, and I am—a doggie dentist.

It is not a pleasant job. Doggie breath is not a fistful of flowers. But it calls to me.

"Wanda!"

Still no response from Wanda, my shiftiest employee, which meant she was still out smoking behind the building, probably standing in the grass, avoiding the doggie piles, and dropping her cigarette butts where she thought I wouldn't see them.

What she doesn't realize is that she's gonna find her butt in a pile of unemployment if she's not careful.

On this particular afternoon, I'd had enough Taco Grande to bloat a hot air balloon. And I'd chewed each bite of mystery beef twenty-five times.

My mama would've been so proud.

I stared at the phone. I stared at the yellow rose wallpaper. I stared at my toothbrush, but instead of picking it up, I tried envisioning the walls in fiesta colors with Mexican smiling moons and suns, brightly-colored murals that would cheer my clientele. Dogs are color-blind, but I swear fun colors make them frolicsome.

And speaking of playful fellas…I thought Keller, my nemesis and fantasy lover, might be feeling frisky right about then, seeing as how he'd probably just finished playing online Texas Hold 'Em with his archenemy, promdate07.

I picked up the phone and dialed. It rang once, twice.

"Hello." A deep shot of southern wild turkey trickled down the line If I listened very carefully, I could hear those rumbly dulcet tones in stereo, seeing as his office was down the hall from mine and both doors were open at that time.

Tingling from the deep vibrations massaging my eardrums, I plunged in.

"I want you to know that I chewed each bite of my food twenty-five times today."

Silence.

"What do you think of that?"

"Feels good, huh?"

The way this man said 'good' made me quiver with unclean thoughts.

"No, it doesn't feel good. I feel like Grandma Moses."

"Grandma Moses." I could hear faint amusement in his words. "Now what's the story with Grandma?"

"You know, the famous artist."

"Hmm." That mellow sound didn't reflect much at all.

"She painted up 'til she was a hundred."

"Sounds like a plan. Keep up the chewing, and maybe you'll live to be a hundred, too."

Keller's inflection never varies. I don't think someone with a register that low has a whole lot of control. It just slides on out, always the same.

Delectable.

"I don't think I can keep it up."

"Sure you can, Tamalyn." There was a brief silence

before his deep chuckle rumbled over the line. "You always do."

I chuckled in response, my own voice huskier than usual.

"Gotta go," he said.

Not yet.

"Keller?" It was so quiet I knew he was still there, just being sneaky.

"What's for supper?" I held my breath, just in case the answer was different today.

"Sardines and crackers."

Dang it.

"Later, Tam."

The phone clicked in my ear. Smarty pants hadn't even waited to hear my usual sign off.

I eased back in my rolling desk chair with the captain's arms and rocked. I loved it 'cause it was the same one Mama used to sit in as she balanced the books for Daddy's paint business. Not comfy, but hers.

"Wanda!"

Still no answer, which meant she'd left early for the day. It was 2:03. Even though we closed at two o'clock on Saturdays, she knew employees weren't supposed to leave until 2:15, just in case something happened to one of our guests—or someone came by with an emergency.

I haven't lost my ever-loving mind. People do have emergencies with their pets, and I'm inclined to help them whenever I get the chance. If you were headed to, say, Hawaii, wouldn't you like your kennel to unlock the door for you if you screeched into the parking lot at 2:01 on your way to the airport? You bet your sweet bippee you would.

I own this shop, the *Drop Your Doggie Inn*. I'm not a vet. Nope. Keller is the vet. These are not his digs, but he stops by every Saturday in his Tony Lama cowboy boots and his Scala straw cowboy hat to give the pets kenneled here a look-see. I don't trust some of the humans that come in here, so it only makes sense for him to give their animals the once over.

What Keller usually does, that's Dr. Keller Stokes to those of you that don't live around here, is check their noses and their mouths. You're thinking cats and dogs, aren't you? Well, I've seen him pry open the mouth of an iguana with a Popsicle stick and check his sharp choppers too. Bless his heart, but the guy has a thing for teeth.

And he does have great teeth, nice and straight and white. A beautiful smile, even if it is on a smallish mouth. Probably a good thing, cause if his smile were any bigger, I would zing into the stratosphere every time he showed that dimple that sits on the left side of his mouth.

I'm not immune to Keller Stokes, even if he and I have known each other from way back in high school. And even if in high school he was the short, plump, freckle-faced boy one year younger than me who asked me to prom. Of course I said, "no," 'cause I was only his *friend* and not his *girlfriend*. Instead, I went with the super-intelligent, way too wealthy Jarrett Davidson, who turned out to be a smart-ass.

How was I to know Keller'd join the Navy and grow the broadest pair of shoulders this side of the Trinity River?

Where was I? Oh, yeah. Now you may be wondering if Keller is a vet, which he is, why he doesn't clean the animals' teeth. Well, that's 'cause I do it before he gets here. I take great pride in my work and in my animals, even the iguanas. I don't want Mr. Sexy Smile to come in, make his small tsk tsking sound, and proceed to clean my clients' teeth.

I pay him to drop by and give 'em a look-see, and that's it. It's worth it, an added service for my dedicated customers, winning brownie points with my new customers. Plus...

You guessed it. I get the unmitigated joy of watching those perfectly creased khakis walk up and down the hall. Sorry, I don't care who you are. No one walks like this ex-Navy officer. His gait is slow and easy, the broad shoulders turning ever so slightly left to right as he saunters along. *Saunters* is the exact word for it too..

I wonder if he's figured out that I clean their teeth before he gets here? Probably.

Probably why he can be the very devil himself. And why he won't ask me out.

"Daydreaming, Tam?"

I jumped out of my skin, shoving my feet off my desk,

hoping to hide my bare legs where my skirt had ridden up. Two hot spots exploded on my cheeks. Argh. I hate it when I blush like that. I'm twenty-six years old, for pity's sake.

"Nope. Planning."

He was on his way out. And it wasn't even 2:15 yet.

"Where's the fire, and what's your hurry?" I said, tilting my chin at him. He wasn't going to figure out from me that he's part of my long-range plan.

"I checked out Bob-a-link and Smudge. They need to come in for their annual check-ups. You'll remind Barbara, right?"

"Sure. Why don't you do it yourself? She should be here any minute."

He looked at me from behind his wire-rimmed glasses. His bright blue eyes blinked a few times, his long blond lashes batting against the lenses, crying out for contacts. Nothing moved on his face for a good four seconds. Then out came the dimple and a small beautiful smile.

"Not tonight, librarian."

I laughed in spite of myself. I don't laugh around Keller as a rule, cause then I get all gushy, and I'm sure he can tell my laughter is way out of proportion to what he's said. Only *I* know it's in exact proportion to what I need—him.

You're probably wondering what he meant by librarian, so I'll tell you. Remember how I said we knew each other from high school? Well, we were both in the drama society. And for our spring musical we presented—you guessed it—*The Music Man*. Yep, I was Marion the Librarian, and he was part of the barbershop quartet, and also my dresser.

Kind of racy, huh? Well, it was very dark, and all I had to do was step out of one dress and into another. Keller merely had to step up and unzip the first one, step back until I was ready, and then step up and zip up the second one. I had on a blouse, a slip, white tights and some matronly shoes. Nothing much to see. But I think he still got a charge out of it.

Heck, I know he got a charge out of it. He asked me to prom, didn't he?

He reached forward to where I still sat behind the desk, a little lightheaded from my over-laughing, and touched his finger to the tip of my nose. "See you tomorrow."

"Don't you mean Saturday?" I expected him to move back as I stood; instead he shot his left dimple at me. It was all I could do not to kiss it.

"Maybe, maybe not."

"Huh." Witty repartee is not my gift.

"Later." He turned, ambling out the door without a second or third glance, the door chimes ringing in his wake.

"Hells, bells, who's at the door?" A chirpy, sarcastic voice screeched.

"Can it, Pollyanna."

The great crimson and emerald bird continued to cry out, oblivious to my disappointment. "Can it, Pollyanna. Can it, Pollyanna."

I hoped maybe this time he'd ask me out. Say something like, 'Hey, how's about some dinner?' But no dice.

Something happened while we were both out in the world, far away from Fort Santa Rosa. He grew broader and stronger and taller. I just grew broader.

Now I'm not saying big girls can't find love, or handsome guys can't love big girls, or big girls and handsome vets can't get together. Cause I'm sure greater miracles than that have happened. I just can't think of any of them.

I'd love to go out and exercise or maybe buy some Lean Cuisines. But I'm not leaving the building these days.

Now I know what you're thinking. You're thinking I work too hard. That's not what I mean. I mean I literally am not leaving the building at all.

I order in.

I wash up in the bathroom.

I sleep in the back.

I've slept in the back since my mama died.

Pitiful. I know. But that was the end. The end of my childhood. You see, my father died several years ago. I've never been married, and I have no children of my own.

Mama and I shared a two-story condo. She had the bottom floor, and I had the top. I haven't cleaned out all of her books and stuff. I haven't cleared off her desk.

Oh, I'm going to very soon. But not just yet.

Not until I'm sure she's not still around. No turning and catching her just out of the corner of my eye. No just about to call out her name and realize she won't answer.

Were we close? We were friends, better friends than mother and daughter.

I've only been sleeping here a couple of weeks. Okay, twenty-one days. But it won't be for very much longer, I'm sure.

No one knows, and it had better stay that way. I don't want to hear any sympathetic comments or be on the receiving end of any sad, pitiful looks from Rose, Wanda, Craig—the dog shampooer—,or Keller.

That's the main thing about to send me over the edge and into outer space. What would Keller think? Heck, I know what he'd think: that I'm absolutely crazy.

But I'm not.

I miss my mama. And I know she misses me. And as soon as I know she's let go of me and this world, then I'll be free to get on back to living in my two-story, uptown condo near the Kroger and the Burger Express.

Excuse me a minute, would ya'?

I'm back. I needed to take a moment and tell her how much I love her. Wanted to reassure her that I won't forget her, and more importantly that I'll be okay. I told her if she wanted to go be with Daddy that was all right by me. But if not, that was okay, too. What else *could* I say? Not sure, but I don't think she was paying close attention.

Well, I think I'll go make sure we're locked up before I give the place a thorough cleaning. I've had to let the cleaning people go for now Don't want them to tell anyone about the big crazy girl who's living in the pet corral on the corner of Taos Road and San Antonio Drive.

My heart is beating so fast I can't think It's eleven o'clock at night, Verizon time, but I could have sworn only a second ago I heard the bells clang on the front door.

Lord, I hope it's not a burglar. I've only got on sweats and a t-shirt, no undergarments—just big ol' me. Heck, it's dark. Who's gonna notice I'm braless while they're robbing the place?

I don't keep cash on hand, at least not over three hundred dollars. Do burglars stop to think about things like that? Nope. They just burgle.

I'd been sleeping in the very last examination room in the back hall, and I realized they might not make it that far. They might stay up front, rifle through the register and the charge receipts, and head on out.

My lord, what if they get into Keller's doggie medications? Some of those are lethal, or at least strong enough to fell an elephant. The good thing about my shop is that it used to be a doctor's office. It has a large waiting area and several examination rooms, plenty of places to separate my guests if a dog's overly rambunctious..

I pressed my ear to the door and heard dogs yapping and parrots squawking. Someone was trespassing. No doubt about it.

I focused, sharp as a tack, or as sharply as I could considering my brain was still in first gear, and my heart was racing. Carefully, I turned the brass handle until the door stood open a mere half inch. I could just make out heavy, slow footfalls at the end of the hall.

They stopped.

I heard what sounded like a door opening. Two seconds passed, and then the door closed with a click. Didn't sound as if whoever it was wanted to keep things quiet. Of course, why would they expect to find anyone in here at this time of night?

The heavy steps clomped down to another examination room, and the next door opened. By this time I had slid to my knees, my spine melting away, like so many M&M's forgotten in my purse.

Hell's bells. They were looking for something. Or someone.

Aw, sh . . . sugar.

I heard whoever it was shut the second door just as carefully as the first and move on to the third room. Something popped into my brain; a plan was starting to take shape.

As soon as the third door opened, I cracked my door enough to scoot my left eye beyond the jamb to see who was coming. I'd left the overhead hall lights off, and the only illumination came from the emergency bulbs over the front desk, several feet away.

The figure was huge, brawny, threateningly calculated in its movements. My heart flew up into my throat. Slowly, I closed the door and waited. As soon as I heard the other door swing shut, I softly closed mine as well. Three rooms down and six to go before whoever it was found me in the very last room of the hall.

Where could I hide until I could run past and call the police?

I opened the lower cabinet doors below the sink, sliding in carefully so my personal parts, which should have been wearing a bra, didn't get caught around the U pipe, then I jammed my back up against the back of the cabinet. Only thing was now I couldn't hear a thing.

Suddenly the cabinet door swung open, and a flashlight nearly blinded me.

"Tamalyn! What the hell are you doing in there?"

A huge, tan hand reached in and pulled. Well, I pulled back. The man—I could sure enough tell it was a man by then—pulled again, unaware of my boob-and-U-pipe problem. Dang it, I didn't ask for this equipment, but, lord, he was about to send me to the hospital.

"Wait a cotton-picking minute!"

The light lowered, and two bright blue eyes peered at me through the sexiest little wire-frame glasses.

"Keller. Oh, my gosh, I thought you were here to skin me alive."

He started pulling again.

"Wait! You're killing me here." As embarrassing as it was, I shifted my boobs around the u pipe and wriggled on out.

"Tamalyn Majors, stand up this minute."

And I did. Hard to ignore an angry, ex-navy vet standing in front of me like a lickable mirage.

As I attempted to gain a steady footing, I fell against his broad chest. He grabbed me by the forearms and righted me. Dang it. He could have pulled me to that slab of pecs and held me. My heart fluttered as if I'd walked

176

too far on an August afternoon, but fear was no longer the reason.

"Steady?"

"Yeah, I guess so."

"Let's go." He turned and marched in front of me, walking me to my court martial, tongue lashing, beating with noodles, or something But I was so tired and keyed up; I didn't care, as long as he was here.

The dogs still snapped and yipped. The parrot cooed, making pleasant little purring sounds it had picked up from one of the cats, the same cat that liked to sit near its cage, fantasizing about the taste of red and green feathers.

I got a good look at Keller. He'd marched us over to the back door that led to the employee parking lot. His eyes blinked, and his small mouth pressed his firm lips together. He propped the door open and walked a couple of steps into the parking lot.

I didn't follow. I was fine right where I was. Besides, I had no shoes on. What was he thinking? I might have cut my foot on a rock or a piece of glass.

"Tamalyn." He sighed, taking off his glasses and cleaning them on the corner of his t-shirt. "What are you doing, Darling?" That incredibly deep voice rolled out, surrounding me like warm arms.

I looked down at my not so attractive sleepwear…and I swear in the light of the glaring fluorescent street lights you could see way too much outline of my boobs. Great!

Crossing my arms over my chest, I piped up. "What are *you* doing? You nearly scared me to death!"

"Tell me you're not sleeping here." Studying his distractingly blue eyes, I saw concern, but I also saw a healthy dose of *'gee, what an idiot!'*

"I'm not sleeping here." I cocked my head to one side, daring him to call me a liar.

His eyes made a leisurely stroll down my body, taking in my soft, comfy sleep pants and matching turquoise shirt. His bright, laser-like gaze flew right back to my face.

Then Keller Stokes did the most amazing thing. He opened his arms, inviting me with his eyes to come in close. My heart fluttered even faster, beating for freedom from my chest, urging me to lay down my worries. I took a tiny step toward him and froze. The gravel-covered parking lot loomed ahead of me; the safety of my office and my animal friends reached out to draw me back inside. Mama, Daddy, and I had created the *Drop Your Doggie Inn* as a haven, and now I was the only one left who remembered why it mattered..

"It's time to go, Darling."

What did he want? Why did he care if I ever stepped into his world?

I raised my chin. "*Why* is it time?" Crossing my arms in front of my chest, I glared at him, my lips twisting with sarcasm.

"You're mama's free, Tamalyn. She's not feeling any pain. She's let this world go, and you with it."

When he said those words, my lungs stopped pumping. I swear they did. How did he know that's what I needed to hear? I hadn't said a word to anyone. The big, squeezable dummy.

Oh, I wanted it so badly to be true. Tears tried to pop out of my eyes, but I refused to let them make an appearance although my chin did quiver a bit. His powerful arms remained open, his eyes glittering with something new. I didn't think he wanted to be my true love. I thought he maybe offered only a warm place for today, for that little fragment of time. And it was enough.

I didn't look down as I took the first step, then another, and another, walking out the doorway into his arms. My head came to rest in the crook of his neck, and his hard, muscled arms crushed me to his chest.

The floodgates opened up inside me, and I leaked big, sloppy tears all over his neck and the front of his shirt. I wiggled my arms free and wrapped them around his waist. Slowly the tears stopped, and still a hoarse keening continued from my dry throat.

Finally, tuckered out from all that freedom, I fell silent, only to hear a short, dry, hiccupping sound coming from the shop. Genevieve, the large grey parrot, had joined me in my misery, producing unattractive, hiccupping sounds of her own. Way to go, Genevieve, old girl.

"Dang, that bird's impressive."

Giggles escaped from my throat, and I searched Keller's face for his reaction to being used as a washcloth and hand towel. Whoa, there was a dimple on one side of that sexy mouth. He laughed a clear bright sound of relief, twirling me around..

"I knew you could do it, Sweetheart." That rolling thunder whisper of approval blew gently in my ear. I swear my leg muscles melted straight away, and I swayed into him.

He swung me up into his arms and headed for his F150.

"Keller Stokes, put me down."

"No way, Sugar. You're coming home with me."

His eyes glinted with confidence and possessiveness.

"But, Keller, the door's standing wide open."

With only a brief hesitation, he tossed me over his shoulder and walked back, pushed in the lock on the knob, and slammed it shut.

He gently lowered me back into his arms, his eyes focused on his black truck, standing like a sentinel in the darkness.

I tapped him on the chin. He just kept walking.

I reached up to that warm, fragrant place in the crook of his neck and bit him.

"Ouch!" His arms tipped, but he didn't set me down. "What was that for?"

"Keller, I'm not wearing a bra. And all my...personal belongings are back in the shop."

"Well, hell, Darling. We can take care of that stuff later." He looked down into my face, clearly not realizing the importance of my foundation garments. "Right now, let's get you home."

"Keller, a fat woman without her undergarments can be a bit frightening. Don't—" I lost myself in the warmth of his lips, and just when I realized it wasn't a dream, he pulled away.

"You're not fat, Tam. And I don't ever want to hear you talk about my girl that way ever again."

I started to argue, but I pinched my lips shut at the stubborn look in his eye. I took a deep breath 'cause there was something I had to ask.

"Keller, why'd you say all that about my mama?"

"Because it's the truth. Darling, I've known you forever. I've seen the sun come out in your smile since the day I heard you sing on that stage at Tate High School. Even though you tried to hide it, I know you've been sick with grief and loneliness."

I'm afraid I sniffed very loudly at that point and slapped his chest. "Keller Stokes, don't you take up with me 'cause you feel sorry for me. I can—"

His mouth came down on mine with such force that the train carrying my thoughts left the station. His arms locked us together with almost superhuman strength, squeezing the arguments right out of me.

That man holds a ton of passion, even if his mouth is kind of on the small side. There's a lot of room to maneuver, and I could lose myself in him if I wanted. Best of all, I discovered there's a well of hopeful laughter within the two of us, enough to make a life full of love.

About the Author

Gina Lee Nelson grew up on the sugar beaches of the Florida Gulf Coast, studied acting on Broadway, married her dark-eyed hero in Central Park, and now calls Texas home. Whether she slung hash as a singing waitress or pounded the streets as a giant Furskin, she's always discovered a way to stand out from the crowd. An active member of Romance Writers of America, she's currently content to express her dramatic nature through her stories and characters.

Reclaiming Tess

by

Beth Shriver

Dedication

To my husband Ty, who doesn't let me quit. There are few men who can wail while they yawn, retort very poor comebacks and encourage me so completely. I love you.

The hills were smaller than she remembered; so was the house. But the big, blue sky seemed to go on forever. Tess left her bags by the ranch house and walked to the huge white barn. Green trim edged its perimeter, and the three Ws brand was etched above the hay loft door.

Nestled in the prairie lands in central Texas, this place felt like Tess's best kept adventure as a kid. With all those years behind her, she couldn't imagine why she had such fond memories of a simple piece of land with a bunch of cows on it.

Then all those memories came flooding back to her. The horse rides, swims in the river and her cousins. She took in a breath of clean country air, stretching her arms out wide and closing her eyes as she inhaled. When she opened them, he was standing right in front of her.

Large dark eyes and hair that fell below his well worn cowboy hat. Wrangler jeans fit loosely over his tall, lean frame, and a white t-shirt hung past his hips. He grinned as he watched her taking him all in.

"Can I help you, Miss?" His grin spread as Tess fumbled for words.

Surprised at her fascination in him, she put one arm down at her side and the other hand on her hip. "I'm Tess Woodson."

"You related to Marcus Woodson?"

Tess paused briefly. "He was my grandfather."

"I'm sorry about Marcus. I had a lot of respect for him. He was a good man to work for."

"Thanks, that's nice to hear."

A third-generation ranch owner, Marcus took great pride in his stock of renowned cattle and horses. He had his first heart attack in his forties and had at least two others his doctor knew about. Tess had secretly been waiting for the call for years. And although it saddened her, she knew when the Lord wanted him, her grandfather was ready to go.

Tess looked around. Some cattle grazed in the west pasture and across the auto gate the horses wandered along the hillside of Sugarloaf Mountain. It wasn't much of a mountain to a Coloradan like her, because these were flatlands. Tall grass and a few wild, yellow roses covered the mound while crickets chirped their song. Meadowlarks swooped down over the tall grasses, nesting and gathering food. The chicken coop bustled with hens, and the sheep wandered in small flocks around the back pasture behind the east barn. All seemed well, but not quite as good as when her grandfather had run the place.

"Everything appears to be running smoothly." Tess was relieved. Knowing things were in good shape here would mean getting back to her job in the city quickly. She didn't want to see her heritage end, but she also knew a dozen summers didn't make her a ranch expert.

He followed her gaze around the barnyard and close by pastures. "It's been a lot of work for the two of us, but we've managed."

Tess whipped her head his way. Grandpa had half a dozen hired hands, more during haying season. This place couldn't run with only two people. "What do you mean *two?*"

He slowly turned to face Tess, his dark eyes studying her. "All the other hired hands are gone. Just Leo and I are left."

Tess felt a sense of panic shoot through her as she stared back at him. She tried not to read too much into this. She'd find a solution. But she had made a vow to call on God now and not try to take it all on her own. This would be a good test.

She paused to regain her composure about her purpose here. This is who she was, and who her grandmother was, and her mother before her, the Woodson women. They were all strong Christian women who had been admired in their time. Would she be like them? Even more so, the question clanging in her head was...would she be admired for loving her Lord?

Sure she'd been successful with her sales position, and the money was good. But when she honestly thought about her life, what was there of any real importance? She was living life like so many others who seemed perfectly happy with their lives. She thought she was happy too, until she was drawn back home and into the relationship she had left behind. The one that had mattered most.

But what did her relationship with God have to do with the ranch? Something kept drawing her here, but she was the last person who should be here. She clenched her fingers together and said a silent prayer. "Why did everyone leave?"

"Your Aunt Levon gave us all a month's pay and said it would be the last. That tends to inspire a person to leave."

Tess scrutinized him. "So why are you still here?" He didn't seem worried. Did that mean he lacked motivation, or was he just truly loyal? By the appearance of the ranch, he was definitely a hard worker.

He took his time answering, studying the place as if he owned it. "I'm not in a hurry. Besides, somebody needs to stick around and take care of these animals."

Tess crossed her arms over her chest. "Did Levon give you any instructions?"

Colt scoffed. "I thought you two struck up a deal."

"We did, but I haven't heard from her since she received my check."

"I see." He shook his head. "I don't think she has a plan as far at the ranch goes. Before you came into play, she said just to auction everything off when she got the go-ahead, including the livestock."

Tess stood speechless, digesting the situation. This wasn't what she'd planned. She pictured it much like her office in Denver: each person should be in their place, doing their jobs, with her overseeing everything. That's the way it was supposed to be. Not one guy, who, although he seemed totally capable, was still only one man. A man who happened to be giving her a smile that about knocked her off her feet.

Tess wished she'd stop staring at him and was really glad when she thought of something to say. "What's your name?"

"Colt Remington."

She grinned. "Remington; how do I know that name?"

"It's a gun."

"So is the name Colt."

Colt lowered his head and then stared up at her. "Let's just say I'm a relative of a guy who made guns."

"Family name?"

"Yeah, most city folk don't figure it out as quickly as you did. I'm impressed."

He looked her up and down. Her Armani sweatsuit and Nylite leather tennis shoes were comfortable on the plane but probably weren't normal attire for a ranch. She pushed back some blond wisps that had escaped her hair clip and realized how uncomfortable she was. She wondered if there were any stores nearby where she could pick up a couple pairs of jeans. The one pair she'd brought weren't fit to be seen; but now, after glancing at Colt's, maybe they were.

"Were your parents always this creative?" She quipped.

"You have no idea."

She wanted to know more about him but didn't want to intrude. He seemed to be a fairly quiet guy but genuine. "So where's Leo?"

"He took the wife and kids into town for dinner."

Tess grinned. "Tubbs?"

Colt returned the smile. "Yeah, I'm sure you know the place."

"Best food within twenty-five miles."

"The *only* food within twenty-five miles."

"That, too." She felt a tinge of enjoyment, but she didn't do that during a crisis. She was a crisis intervention specialist, and having two hired hands to work a 7,000-acre ranch qualified as a crisis.

"If you're hungry, I can take you into town." Colt brought her back with his deep, slow drawl.

Her hesitation became obvious when she stuffed her hands into her pockets, so he continued.

"You could meet Leo and his family."

"I know Leo. He's been working the ranch since I was a kid. I'm glad to hear he and Jen have a child now."

"Two to be exact, twins."

Tess nodded. "I'd like to stay and get a feel for the place." She gestured toward the horse stables. She'd always had a passion for horses, but Grandpa bred a fine stock, so, consequently, she'd only been allowed to ride a select few.

"I'll be in the bunkhouse if you need me." He tipped the brim of his hat with one finger then turned away.

Tess thanked him and began the short walk toward the horse barn. She heard him kick up gravel with each step as he walked toward his small white home near the ranch house. She wanted to watch him go but thought better of it. Then she changed her mind and took a fleeting glance his way. He had just turned his head toward her, and their eyes locked for a split second. She quickly looked away. She should have listened to her first instinct, which she hoped was God telling her not to get involved with this guy. The last thing she needed was to become interested in someone who probably only had a high school education.

****

What kind of irony is this, Lord? Colt walked down the dirt road leading to the bunkhouse. The dull yellow sun had almost disappeared behind the grasslands to the west. He stopped to admire it and noticed how the Woodson land seemed to go on forever. And from where he was standing, it did. *God's reminder of his creation made for us to enjoy with Him.*

He tugged at the brim of his hat and stared at the pebbled ground beneath him. He moved his boot over the small rocks, in thought. It had only been a few months since Annie had left him. After a year with him, she had tired of trying to get him off the ranch and into a *real* job. A *career*, she'd called it. Annie only called one time, to tell him where she'd gone and to see if he'd made any changes. Months had passed, and he knew she'd moved on and given up on him. Maybe Annie was right not to want a ranch hand for a husband. But if she really loved him, wouldn't she have stayed?

Now with everything in place, the timing was right to leave as he'd planned. It must not have been God's plan, because in walked a gorgeous blond with a quick mind and a taste for the country. He took in the crisp night air and wondered if a big-city, corporate woman like Tess would even consider a ranch hand like him.

He finished the short walk to the small white house

he'd called home for the last two years. He loved growing up in the country, but thought it wise to get a college degree. He'd missed the country and come back home afterward, and found work at this ranch. This ranch he had come to love.

Colt popped open the screen door and dropped his hat onto the kitchen table. He opened a window for some fresh air, then looked out toward the ranch house, Tess's house now. He chuckled, why was he even hesitating to leave now? Her interest in him was purely business. She needed information about the ranch, and he had what she needed.

****

Although they still needed more help, with the new hired hands they'd found, the place was starting to run smoothly. Leo taught those with farm experience the routine with the daily chores. Colt and the other hired hands who knew ranch work helped with the horses and cattle. The others made daily runs around fence lines and dropped off salt blocks by the windmills. They all worked to maintain the buildings and machinery.

Tess began to understand how best utilize each man's abilities. She learned how to integrate her corporate skills into a team of ranch hands instead of a team of sales reps.

And then there was Colt, incredibly devoted to the ranch, and to her. He introduced Tess to the ways of the ranch in such a way she felt herself falling in love with the land, and maybe Colt too. Nothing much seemed to faze the earthy cowboy. She'd learned to accept his compliments without reservation, even if he was just being a nice guy. Like when she got bucked off the most gentle horse on the ranch, and couldn't herd a cow to save her life.

As if on cue, Tess turned to see Colt standing on the porch. His broad shoulders faced the door as he stared out over the barn yard. When he turned to the side, Tess decided he looked good from all angles.

"Morning." He gave her the once over, but not in the way guys in the city did. His was innocent and well meant, literally as she found out. "You ready to ride?"

She shook her head. "Oh no, I'll leave that to you and

Leo. I think I need to take some lessons or something."

He tilted his head forward, motioning to the kitchen. "Have you eaten breakfast?"

Tess remembered how important it was for the ranch hands to eat their three square meals every day. Meals were sacred and made by women like Jen and her grandmother, women who spent their entire day cooking, cleaning and preparing for the next meal.

"Well, yeah. But I'm not dressed."

He looked her up and down again. "You're not?"

She glanced down at the hole in her sagging jeans and the stain in her old sweatshirt. "I've never worn this out in public before."

He shrugged and put his hands in his pockets. "You look just fine to me," he said with a twinkle in his eye. That was all it took. She slipped on her shoes and followed him to the barn in no time.

****

Tess hung up the phone and walked into the family room. "Sorry, Grandma was on a roll tonight. She's still upset with the way Grandpa left the finances regarding the ranch."

Colt moved to the end of the couch. "Why is she so bitter?"

Tess sighed and sat next to the fire. "Grandpa put the ranch first. Grandma, along with everyone else, came after. I understood it was just his way, so did my dad and Aunt Levon, but it took its toll on Grandma."

Colt took a sip of his coffee, feeling the burn on his tongue. "I can understand that in a way. But I can also identify with your grandfather."

Tess tilted her head as if studying him. He knew what she was thinking and knew he should explain himself. "When you work a ranch, you know it like you do a person. You rise with it every day and sleep knowing it's there for you to tend to the next day. It consumes you, and it nurtures your soul as much as you care for the land."

Tess furrowed her brows. Maybe he had gotten a little too poetic and should back up a bit. "I do understand your grandmother feeling the way she did, but why carry it around with her now? Marcus isn't even around anymore to be mad at."

"Just old wounds, I guess."

"Wounds she keeps open."

Tess nodded. "That's true." She pulled the wool blanket up and around her. "When you were talking about the land, what land were you talking about?"

"I felt that way about the farm when I was growing up. It gets in your blood, or it doesn't. For some people there's no other way of life."

"But now you mean this land." She turned her head to meet his eyes.

"Yeah, now it's this land." He chuckled. "Do I sound crazy?"

"Not at all. As a matter of fact, you've made me feel completely sane for becoming so attached to this place again."

Colt felt a glimmer hope. "Do you think you might stay?"

Tess shook her head. "I have a good-paying job back in Denver." She shrugged. "I don't know how I could."

Colt looked down at his hands and laced his fingers together. He was glad she appreciated it here as much as he did. But would she continue to feel this way?

Tess seemed to be waiting for Colt to respond; when he didn't she added, "I'll just have to pray about it and see where He leads me."

Knowing Tess leaned on God made Colt's heart take off like a herd of wild mustangs. "It's hard work to run a ranch. It's all-consuming and would be a completely different way of life for you."

"I know, but if it's where the Lord wants me, I'll stay."

Colt nodded. "I feel that same way about this land as I do with God. That He's a part of you just like this land is."

Tess shifted to the side and averted her eyes. "I used to know that feeling."

"But not anymore?"

She shook her head. "It's starting to come back to me."

Colt was familiar with her feelings. He'd been there and made the long journey back. He wanted to comfort her in knowing that God would come back to her, that

He'd never really left. He pushed himself up and leaned forward. He raised a hand to her back, almost touching her, then thought better of it and pulled his hand away.

"Being here helps. There is some sort of truth in what you said, about the land and if it means something to you, what it can do to your soul."

"So you really didn't think I was crazy?" he teased.

When she grinned, his heart melted like the snow on a warm spring day.

"No, I can relate too well. That's why I'm here."

Colt gazed into her gray stormy eyes and saw the passion there. She wanted this land, maybe as much as he did. And she's smart enough to know to keep it. This was a woman he could fall in love with.

****

Colt had been working with a new horse for hours. His shirt was drenched in sweat. He removed his hat and raked his fingers through his wet hair then walked over to the first corral, where Tess sat waiting on top of the fence.

She watched Colt stick his head into the horse trough and then whip it back. Streams of water flew into the air and splashed down on the dirt. He shook his head back and forth until his hair lifted into large curls around his head and face. Colt turned to her as he placed his hat firmly on his head. "What are you smiling about?"

"I've never seen anyone wash their hair quite like that before."

He smiled back. "You might be doing it yourself one of these days."

"That'll be the day."

"You wanna bet on it?"

"Do you wanna lose?"

"And if you lose, you trough wash your hair." He held out his hand. "What's the bet?"

"That I can keep this place running. I know no one thinks I can."

He put his hand down and leaned forward to take off his spurs. "We'd both be betting on the same thing. I guess we'll have to wait until we can find something we don't agree on before we can make that bet."

Tess felt the temperature rise in her cheeks, but she

didn't care. She felt incredibly touched by his simple words that meant so much to her.

After being at odds with most everyone all the time at work, it was nice to have someone on her side. Actually, two. She knew God had a master plan in all this. If she could just learn to be co-captain again, she felt she'd be pleasantly surprised with the outcome.

"I appreciate that, Colt."

"I wouldn't say it if I didn't mean it."

"I know you did." He said it with his eyes, those eyes that spoke a thousand words. As Tess stared at him, she asked God what in the world she was supposed to do.

****

Colt knocked and walked into the kitchen where Tess sat with a pad and pen in her hand. She looked better every time he saw her. She wore less makeup, if any. Her wardrobe was casual, unlike the designer coordinates she wore when she first came to the ranch. She didn't fuss with her hair either. A ponytail or braid was her new style, and gave her a natural appeal.

He took a seat next to her and glanced over at the piece of paper she'd written on. "Are you working?"

"Always. I've realized how demanding my job is even more since I've been here. Makes me wish I could stay on the ranch."

Colt couldn't contain the rush that swelled in his gut. He had been trying to get up the nerve to ask her how she felt about him. He'd prepared himself either way, but he had reached the point that he had to know one way or another if they had a chance together. But now he wondered if it was the right time. She had to make one tough decision, she didn't need two.

"You seem surprised." Tess put a hand to her chin.

"I guess I have mixed emotions."

She pinched her eyebrows together and turned away. He wished he could spit out a few more words to explain himself better, but his mind stayed on overload. Thoughts of Annie came roaring back to him like a thundering stampede. He couldn't go through that again, especially with Tess.

She let out a breath. "It would be the worst career move possible, but I just can't bring myself to leave."

Colt tried to stifle his excitement at having her there with him. But if he really cared about her he had to think of what was best for her, not himself. "I think I'm the wrong person to talk to about this."

Tess squinted. "Your opinion is the only one I care about."

Colt threw that around his mind like a lasso, trying to make sense of it. "Why me?"

Tess smiled tenderly. "Because you're one of the reasons I want to stay."

How he'd longed to hear those words. But if worse came to worse he didn't want to be the blame for it. "I had planned on leaving once things were on track here, but nothing's definite."

Tess averted her eyes. He felt his heart thud in his chest. He didn't want to be the only reason for her to stay. This was too hard of a life if you didn't love the country. But looking at her now he didn't know if he could hold back. "What are you working on?"

Her eyes lifted as she picked up the pad. "It's a proposal for work, and my finances." She cringed. "It costs a lot to run this ranch."

"I'll do whatever I can to help you with the proposal." The knot in Colt's stomach tightened when Tess gave him a blank stare. He couldn't tell if she looked shocked, angry, or hurt by his comment, but something stirred inside that pretty head.

Colt tipped his grin to one side. "I guess I didn't tell you I went to college. Proposals were my specialty." They weren't really, but if it would help her out, he'd make it work.

Tess opened her mouth, but it took a while for anything to come out. "I didn't know..."

Colt let it sink in with a nod.

"College?"

"University of Texas." Simple was better since she seemed so surprised.

She gave a nod, and her eyes came back into focus. Maybe he could use more than one-word sentences now. "Well...," Tess's brows lifted with confusion. "I appreciate your offer, but no. I'm tired anyway. I think I'll turn in for the night." She stood abruptly and crossed her arms over her chest.

He felt the chill of her words like a frozen river in the winter, and fought for something to say. She seemed sad at his response when she asked him about staying on the ranch, and now she seemed mad about his education.

He sincerely hoped she felt stronger about this way of life than the one she came from. Maybe he was wrong not to tell her how he really felt. He seemed to be *really* wrong telling her about college. Colt sighed inwardly. He couldn't win.

****

Tess jumped at the unexpected knock at the ranch house door. Colt's handsome face beamed at her from the other side of the window. She felt a soft flutter in her chest as she gazed into his warm, brown eyes.

She had his coffee with fresh cream waiting for him, and as she handed it to Colt, Tess felt as if she were with someone she had known for many years.

The casual comfort of being by his side made everything feel whole and good again. She felt the tension from yesterday melting away. She waited for the awkwardness to set in, but it never came, and she felt the same comfort coming from Colt. They sipped their coffee and made plans for their day. She wanted to know everything about the ranch, even the small details.

"So did Jen and Grandma decide where Christmas dinner will be?" Jen and Tess's Grandma unintentionally created a rivalry to determine who the best cook is on the Woodson ranch. This had lead to some stressful decision-making and tongue-tied hired hands, but excellent food.

"Yeah, it started as a standoff at first, but they ended up compromising." Colt chuckled. "Leo put them in the milk barn, so they could be on neutral territory until they reached an agreement. It was mighty cold in there, so I think they hurried things along. We're going to have Christmas at Tubb's."

"What? I can't believe it. I remember Grandpa going there after the divorce for holidays, but for those two to agree that neither one of them make a holiday dinner?"

"I think it turned out to be more that they agreed to

196

disagree, and this was the only compromise they could come up with."

"Well, at least it's settled."

"No one's said a word about it. We're all just glad they've decided to eat a meal together."

Tess laughed. "Two talented ladies, letting their stubbornness get in the way."

"They'd be a great team if they ever set aside their pride."

"Oh, can you imagine?"

Everything seemed so simple here. Finding enough hired hands was the worst of her problems, so she had to work harder, not a loss on the sales or an irate customer to schmooze over, just old-fashioned hard work.

And she felt God here. He existed all around her, in nature and living off the land. She didn't say anything for a few seconds, soaking it all in. And then, "Thank you," popped out.

Colt's smile started slowly but widened into the biggest smile she'd seen. His brown eyes darkened and softened. "For what?"

"Helping me make a decision."

Colt's stare showed his concern. "About last night.... I hardly slept a wink..."

She put a hand on his arm. "It's okay. I was hurt at first. That you hadn't told me about your business degree and that you didn't ask me to stay. But then I realized I'd asked the wrong person. I could tell how you felt about me the minute I met you. It took me longer to get past my expectation of who I thought I was supposed to be with and start listening to God instead."

"Well, I hope He's been telling you what I've been asking Him to." Then he gave her that grin, the one he gave her the first day they met. The one that about knocked her off her feet. "I might be wrong, but I think you should give it a chance here. And with me."

She felt the barrier fall away, creating an opening to start a relationship with him. Tess looked down at the words on the paper she had written, facts and figures. "I've been praying about where God wants me to be, so between you and Him, I guess I'm going to have to trust you both."

****

Another chilly day took its toll on the ranch. When the wind picked up, it was almost unbearable. The windmills spun around as if their tops would fly off, and the cattle sought protection behind the hills.

Colt and Tess sat at the large kitchen table where the ranch hands had their meals. "There's nothing good about this day." Tess pouted as she flipped through the pages of an unread book.

Colt finished his breakfast, wiped his mouth with a napkin and leaned over the table. He hadn't seen her in such a melancholy mood before. "Why would you say that? Just because the wind's blowing?"

Tess scoffed. "I wish that was it." She let out a breath. "We still don't have enough hired hands. I don't have a job..."

He grinned at her and, his head cocked to the side, listened to her whine.

She smiled weakly. "And the wind's blowing."

He took her hand and kissed it, enjoying the soft silkiness of her skin. "Your job is here, the wind will stop blowing and I'll find some more hands."

Tess's eyes widened. "I can't let you do that. You don't have the money any more than I do."

He started to say something but stopped himself. He hadn't told anyone about the investments he'd made, and didn't want to now; he just wanted her to trust him. "You've already used all your stocks to save this ranch. If I can help out with hiring some hands let me worry about where the money comes from."

"I wish I could, but I can't. Whoever has the deed runs the ranch." She turned up a lip. "I guess you and Leo run the ranch, but that's why it's even more important that I take care of the finances."

He gave up, knowing she wouldn't budge. So he held up his hands. "Okay, but if you change your mind..."

"I appreciate it, Colt. But I can't." She stroked his arm with her fingers.

Colt melted at her tender smile and warm touch. Her gray eyes seem to glow with admiration as she fixed her gaze on him.

"I know you wouldn't be so stubborn as to let the

ranch go due to your pride." That would make her think. He knew it did. Sometimes he had to say things like that to get her to give her decisions more thought. To remind her that it wasn't like it used to be when she had to fend for herself in the business world.

"I swallowed that a long time ago." Her eyes looked peaceful and her voice was soft.

Colt's heart soared like a prairie hawk at her words. Now he needed to lower his pride, and ask her what he'd been meaning to since he first laid eyes on her.

****

The snow started falling and didn't stop until the crystal, white flakes covered the entire countryside. It meant more work for the hands, but they welcomed the snow because the river was the main water source for all of the livestock. And although windmills were used, the water was frozen and had become useless to the cattle.

Colt sat next to Tess in the old sleigh he'd refurbished. The feel of him close to her created tingles, and feelings long forgotten. It seemed natural for him to be there, right beside her. He got the horses going with brisk tones and the familiar words used by her grandfather. She watched how the leather reins intertwined through his gloved fingers and how he moved each hand separately to adjust the horses to move in a synchronized rhythm.

"Give it a try." He handed the reins to her. The horses were trotting a straight path with not much adjusting so it wasn't necessary to do much.

Tess gave Colt the reins and sat back against the wooden seat. Colt rounded the corner behind the dam and stopped in front of a huge evergreen tree. It had a four-foot circumference at the bottom and reached close to eighteen feet high. But the most fascinating thing about it was its perfect shape, as if someone had trimmed it.

Tess sat back and enjoyed the vast amount of green against a backdrop of white. "What a great Christmas tree."

"I thought this would cheer you up." Colt dropped the reins and sat back with her. "We could save a tree every year and just come out and decorate this one." He put his arm behind Tess and blew out a white cloud into the air.

She felt a warm reaction in her chest when she noticed his full lips and thought about how they felt against hers. She watched the cloud disappear and appreciated his thoughtfulness. How did he know exactly what she would like? She would rather be here admiring this tree than going to any four-course dinner party or the latest play on Broadway as in her past life. And that's exactly how she began to see things, as the before and after life. The few years in big business, without God, and the one she lived now in the country, with Colt, on her grandfather's land, getting to know her heavenly Father again.

The night was clear, and the stars were bright. They looked for a shooting star but would get carried away in conversation and forget. They would be reminded when a glimmer of light would catch their eye. The thermos of hot chocolate had disappeared long ago, along with the sugar cookies Tess had made. They'd spent a lot of time reminiscing over the changes that had taken place since Tess had come to the ranch.

Tess shifted closer to him and heard a creak in the old wooden seat. "We've had a lot of changes over such a short time. I'd like things to slow down a little." Tess gazed into the twinkling sky as she spoke.

"My city girl wants things to slow down?" Colt chuckled. "You'd get bored."

She smiled at his insight. He was probably right. "Well, I would like a couple more things to happen." She leaned closer and looked into his eyes.

"Like getting hitched?"

Tess felt a flood of emotion come over her. "I guess that was an offer."

"I told you proposals were my specialty."

She hugged his arm. "And you want an answer?"

He nodded with a raised brow and half a smile.

Tess threw her arms around his neck and kissed him passionately. Colt dropped the reins. The horses would have to find their own way home.

About the Author

Beth Shriver is a writer whose works are published in non-fiction periodicals and books. Her stories include young adult, historical, romance and women's fiction.

Bounty Hunting, Texas Style

by

Arline Todd

Dedication

This is for Mariah Allane and Daniel Anthony,
the two youngest members of my family,
who just happen to be born in Texas.
Both are _all things bright and beautiful_.

Nicole Beaumont set her Louis Vuitton suitcase onto the Italian marble floor of the foyer at her aunt's Highland Park mansion.

The butler immediately took the bag in his hand. "Welcome to Texas, Miss Beaumont. We weren't expecting you. Mrs. Parker said you would be unable to attend the charity ball."

"I had a change of plans, so I came down on the company Lear at the last minute. I know it's late. Is my aunt still awake?"

"Yes, ma'am. Mrs. Parker is in the library, reading. Go right in. I'll take your luggage to your room."

"Thank you, Kenneth." Nicole strode past the fragrant arrangement of yellow roses gracing a mahogany table centered between the two staircases leading to the upper floors, her heels clicking on the marble floor. The library, her aunt's favorite room, stretched along the back of the mansion and its windows looked out on the patios and lush gardens behind the house.

She drew a deep breath and opened the library's double doors. She couldn't put it off any longer. She was here now; there was no turning back. She had dreaded this moment ever since she left Virginia. During the entire flight, she worried about how to handle it. How could she hurt her aunt like this? But how could she not? She had to cooperate with the law.

Nothing had changed since her last visit. The furniture gleamed, the scent of fresh flowers filled the air, and her portrait still hung in the place of honor over the fireplace mantle. She saw her aunt curled up on the large padded armchair, a book in her hands. Nicole felt a sharp pang somewhere around her heart. Not only was Evelyn Parker her aunt, but she had also filled the roles of mother and father to her after her own parents were killed in a car accident when she was sixteen.

Evelyn looked up and smiled at her. "Darlin', what a nice surprise! I'm so glad you changed your mind about attending the charity ball." She left her book on the coffee table and went to her niece. "I've missed you so much, Sweetheart."

"Oh, Aunt Ev," Nicole whispered as she embraced her aunt, "I have bad news."

Almost overcome by the stress she'd dealt with all day, Nicole felt her eyes burn with tears. She held back her emotions by sheer force of will as her aunt held her at arm's length and studied her face. Her aunt gave a slight frown.

"Sweetheart, are you ill?"

"I'm fine." Nicole lied.

"No, you're not. You're as pale as a summer cloud. Sit down. If you're well, nothing else matters. Whatever it is, we'll take care of it." She guided Nicole to the sofa and tilted her face up with a finger. "Tell me what's wrong, Darlin'?"

Nicole inhaled deeply and forced herself to relax against the cushions. "I'm here to arrest your godson."

"What?"

"There's an outstanding warrant for his arrest. He's wanted for embezzling nine million dollars from the Richmond division of Grayson Enterprises. He ignored a court order to turn himself in to the Richmond authorities. I'm so sorry, Ev. I know how close you are to him."

Evelyn leaned back against the cushions and patted Nicole's hand. "It's all right. Obviously, it's a mistake of some kind. Kyle wouldn't embezzle money from his own company. Nicole, you must know nine million is a drop in the bucket to Kyle. He's a billionaire! And, more importantly, he's a Southern gentleman."

Nicole managed not to groan aloud. "I know. But I have a warrant. I can't ignore it. That's why I came." Nicole eyed her aunt. Didn't she realize how many people got rich by embezzling money under their control? No, of course she didn't.

"Darlin', you can't arrest my godson in my own home."

Nicole stood and began pacing. "I know this presents a problem. You can't imagine how I dreaded telling you." Nicole slipped off her jacket and tossed it onto the back of a chair. She winced when Evelyn gazed reproachfully at the Glock she wore in a shoulder holster.

"I forbid it, Nicole. You'll just have to arrest him somewhere else. And it will have to be *after* the charity ball. He's the host! He's sponsoring it to raise money for the Grayson Children's Hospital and Research Center. *His* hospital, Darlin'. He built it."

Nicole sighed. For the past two years, every time she talked to her aunt, Evelyn managed to bring Kyle Grayson into the conversation. He hung the moon and the stars. He was a genius, a philanthropist without peer, the most loving godson in the whole wide world. Nicole bit her lip. Evelyn obviously loved him. "There is a risk, Ev. Some brutal bounty hunter could show up and arrest him. At least with me, he'll get treated with respect. And no rough stuff." *If he cooperates,* she added to herself.

Evelyn's frown deepened. Nicole could almost see the wheels turning in her aunt's mind as Evelyn considered the matter.

"You have a point, Sweetheart. We'll warn Kyle. He can go right to you to be arrested if he has to. I'll explain the problem to him. He should be here any minute."

"Here?" Nicole felt her jaw drop.

"We're going over some last-minute details for the ball. I think you should go on up and unpack while I explain." Her aunt's gaze went to the doorway as a male voice drifted to them. "Oh dear, it's too late now," Evelyn said.

Nicole looked toward the doorway at the man paused on the threshold. She knew Kyle Grayson was handsome. Evelyn had bombarded her with photos of her beloved godson. But the photos hadn't done him justice. In person, he was stunning. His dark hair was almost black, and he had the face of an archangel.

"Dear boy, I'm so glad to see you!" Evelyn beckoned him into the room. "Nicole is here and I can finally introduce you."

Nicole held out her hand as Evelyn went through the formalities. She could swear she felt a sizzle zip up her entire arm as she clasped his hand.

"Hello, Nicole. I've been dying to meet you ever since I saw your portrait." His gaze flicked over her and rested for just a moment on her holstered gun.

Nicole saw that his eyes were a mesmerizing midnight blue, and his deep, velvet-smooth voice almost finished her. The Pied Piper would have killed for a voice like that. She took a deep breath and composed herself. "Oh, thanks, but that was painted many years ago, just before I left for college. I think of it as my Grace Kelly look—sweet and demure. I'm really nothing like her." She was proud of the light, casual tone she managed to achieve. "And I come bearing bad news."

Kyle smiled and raised one eyebrow. "Bad news?"

"We'll explain, Dear," Evelyn spoke before Nicole had a chance to break the news. "Let's sit down."

Nicole and Kyle sat on opposite ends of the sofa facing the armchair in which Evelyn had been reading. Nicole launched into a brief explanation and then took a sheaf of papers from her briefcase and handed them to Kyle.

As he studied the material, a slight frown warring with the bewildered look on his face, Nicole could have sworn he was genuinely surprised.

Kyle shook his head and looked her directly in the eyes. "It's a mistake of some kind."

"That's what I told her," Evelyn said, her voice laced with satisfaction. "Call your lawyers and let them straighten this out."

"I will." Kyle frowned and looked at Nicole. "Am I under arrest?"

Nicole opened her mouth to answer him, but her aunt cut her off yet again. "Of course not. I explained to Nicole about the charity ball you're sponsoring. She understands. You just have to stay close to her until after the ball and then she'll arrest you officially, unless your lawyers have fixed the mistake. Nicole will protect you against the bounty hunters."

Nicole had to smile at the mixture of confusion and horror that flickered over Kyle's face.

"Bounty hunters are after me?" His eyes darkened. "You're a bounty hunter? I thought your company specialized in high-risk security situations."

"We do. We rarely get involved in bounty hunting, but someone sent me an anonymous tip about your warrant. That's why I'm here."

He nodded. "I appreciate your understanding. I have no idea how this happened. I assure you I'm not an embezzler." He smiled. "Word of honor."

"Of course you're not," Evelyn asserted and reached over the coffee table to pat his hand.

Nicole mentally rolled her eyes.

Kyle grinned. "Thanks, Ev. But this is serious. If word gets out, I'll have one hell of a time convincing people to donate the big bucks we need for the new wing at the hospital."

Nicole watched him carefully while he called his attorneys and instructed them to "get this mess cleaned up and keep it confidential." He must be paying them a hefty retainer, she thought. The attorney he called didn't seem to object one bit to being called at home at such a late hour.

Nicole stood. "Well, Ev, I'm going to turn in. I'll see you in the morning." She looked at Kyle as he snapped his cell phone shut. "Good night, Kyle."

"Good night," he replied. "And thanks again for your help."

"You sleep in, Darlin'. Kyle will stay here tonight and we can all go to an early lunch tomorrow."

Nicole kissed her aunt's cheek and started down the hall toward the stairs, but stopped when she heard Ev's question.

"What do you think of my girl, Dear?"

Nicole tiptoed back to the partially open doors and peeked through the crack near the hinges. Kyle was looking at the painting over the fireplace and turned to her aunt with a smile.

"I fell in love with the woman in the painting years ago. Her angelic beauty really got to me. But the flesh-and-blood Nicole is so much more. She's not only beautiful and intelligent, but, God bless her, she's also *dangerous*. Who could resist that combination?"

Evelyn laughed. "I knew you'd like her, Dear," she said with satisfaction. She patted his arm. "Let's call it a night. We can go over the ball details in the morning."

Nicole, her face flushed with embarrassment, slipped out of her noisy high-heels and hurried down the hall and up the staircase to her room. She was ashamed of herself for eavesdropping on her aunt and Kyle. What was wrong with her? Why did she get so flustered over a mild instant attraction? That's all it was. Well, maybe the mild part was wrong. It was more of an explosive instant attraction. But what really bothered her was all this talk of mistakes. He was probably acting the innocent. Warrants didn't get issued by mistake. He was as guilty as sin. But he was also an irresistible hunk, a drop-dead gorgeous hunk. Nevertheless, she was going to take him to jail after that charity ball tomorrow night, instant attraction notwithstanding.

When she finally went to bed, she had a hard time getting to sleep, tossing and turning most of the night. She woke late the next morning and rang for juice and coffee to be brought to her room. She showered quickly then chose a powder blue suit, specially tailored to allow for her shoulder holster, and a pale yellow blouse that went well with the highlights in her hair.

While she nibbled on the pastries that accompanied the beverages, Nicole called her office in Virginia to make sure things were running smoothly.

"Do you need some backup?" her assistant asked.

It was tempting, but she'd be taking Grayson back to Virginia on the Lear early tomorrow morning. She hated to pull a man off one of the contracts in process. It would be a scheduling nightmare. "I can manage. It's just one more day. I'll see you tomorrow. Call me if anything urgent comes up."

Later, downstairs, she found her aunt and Kyle in the living room talking to a boy. Both Kyle and the boy stood when she entered the room. Well, she thought, some of the Southern manners were quite nice.

"Nicole, this is my protégé, Jeffery Miller. He'll be working in my computer room this afternoon," Evelyn said.

The boy blushed and awkwardly shook the hand Nicole held out to him. Since she had gone through a shy period of her own when she was a teenager, she felt a spurt of sympathy for him. He was a clean-cut boy dressed like a typical teenager in faded jeans with small rips and holes scattered about and a T-shirt, but instead of Nikes, he sported a scuffed pair of cowboy boots. Oh well, this was Texas after all. Maybe cowboy boots were the in-thing with the teenage crowd.

She smiled at him. "It's nice to meet you, Jeffery. So you're interested in computers?"

Jeffery flushed a deeper shade of red. "Oh, yes ma'am."

Evelyn patted the boy's arm. "You go on up, Dear. Stay as late as you can. I'll see you tomorrow."

After Jeffery practically fled from the room, his boots clicking on the marble tiles when he reached the foyer, Evelyn spoke in a low tone. "He's a good boy. Quite brilliant. He can make a computer do everything but walk the dog."

Kyle laughed. "And his family can't afford the state-of-the-art equipment you have or the education you're underwriting."

"He's a prodigy. And you know how I feel about wasting brilliant minds."

Kyle kissed her cheek. "Yes, I do."

"Also, it's a little payback for the millions my late husband and I made from computer innovations," Evelyn added.

"You're a soft touch, Aunt Ev," Nicole teased.

"Always have been," Evelyn admitted. "A Southern gentlewoman prides herself on helping others."

Nicole grinned. "Please don't ever change."

"You don't have to worry about that. Now, while I see to the packing, Kyle can fill you in on what his lawyers have found out."

Nicole felt as if she'd lost track of something. "Packing?"

"Kyle has arranged for a suite for us at the Gaylord Texan Resort. That's where the ball is being held tonight. It's more convenient than having to come back here and then go out to Grapevine again. Did you bring a gown, Darlin'?"

"No, but I have a black dress in my emergency suitcase. It should be okay."

Evelyn laughed. "No, that won't do. Think Academy Awards. But don't worry; I have just the thing for you. It was going to be a Christmas surprise, but I can get something else."

Nicole took a seat on the sofa and grimaced as she heard her aunt laughing again as she closed the door behind her. "Academy Awards?"

Kyle sat down on the opposite end of the sofa. "It's very formal. Tuxedos for men. Formal gowns for the ladies. Dinner. Orchestra. Dancing. Entertainment. You'll love it."

"Humph. You think?"

"Sure."

Nicole shrugged and changed the subject. "What did your attorneys find out?"

Kyle frowned. "The warrant is valid. I don't know what to think. Someone took the money and I assume that someone cooperated in an investigation, since charges were brought against me. And then this same person intercepted all the legal paperwork sent to me. I'm being set up somehow."

Nicole tried to ignore his sexy voice and concentrate on what he was saying. "Do you have enemies?"

"Unfortunately, I do. Some with real gripes, others with imagined ones."

"What do your attorneys recommend?"

"They're going to send a team directly to the Virginia facility and try to get to the bottom of this. They should be leaving sometime this evening, so they'll be there tomorrow when you and I arrive in Richmond. Hopefully, they can keep me out of jail and keep the whole mess away from the media." He turned to face her, studying her somberly. "I appreciate your restraint."

There was a hint of challenge in the lift of her chin. "I'm doing it for my aunt."

His beautiful voice gentled. "I know that. I'm still grateful."

The door opened and Evelyn called to them. "We're all set to go. The car's loaded and I'm hungry."

Relieved to have her conversation with Kyle at an end, Nicole followed her aunt to the car, and Evelyn motioned her to sit in the front with Kyle, while she sat in back. Evelyn told them she wanted to have lunch at her favorite family restaurant. She gave Kyle directions from the back seat, pointing out the sights to Nicole as they went.

"Here it is." Kyle parked the car and opened his door.

Nicole reached for the door handle on her side of the car, but stopped when Evelyn leaned forward and placed a hand on her shoulder.

"Wait, Dear. You're in Texas now."

Of course, Nicole thought, how could I forget? She smirked as Kyle opened her door and held out his hand to assist her. For a fleeting moment, she considered not taking his hand, but that would bother Evelyn, so she ignored the sizzle she felt when their hands touched as he guided her out of the car.

He smiled, and his eyes twinkled as his gaze flicked to the slight bulge of her holstered Glock.

Her lips tightened. She just knew what he was thinking—it was ironic to have to be polite and assist a "helpless" female who also happened to be armed.

As they walked toward the entrance to the restaurant, Kyle's cell phone rang and he dropped back a few steps to take the call. "Go ahead. I'll be right behind you."

Nicole glanced toward the door and made eye contact with an elderly man dressed in a suit and crowned with a large cowboy hat. Even though she and Evelyn were a good hundred feet from the doorway, the man stepped back and patiently held the door, waiting for them.

Oh, God, she thought. Being in Texas is like being in a foreign land where the minutia of daily living was strange.

Evelyn gave a gracious nod to the man as she passed him, and he tipped the rim of his cowboy hat to her.

The hostess came to them.

"A table for three, please," Evelyn said.

"This way, ma'am."

Evelyn followed behind the hostess and Nicole was happy to trail along behind in their wake.

Kyle caught up with them in time to hold Evelyn's chair, which gave Nicole a chance to scoot around the table and seat herself. She flipped open her menu and gave it a cursory glance, then looked around the restaurant while the others perused their menus. She had the impression of a lot of brown wood brightened by red and white checked tablecloths and murals on the walls.

Several of the tables had toddlers in high chairs. This was definitely a family restaurant. And then her gaze hit a two-line phrase painted across the entire back wall in huge letters:

Born American by Accident of Birth

Born Texan by the Grace of God

She could hardly believe her eyes. Only in Texas would you see something like that. "Look at the sign!"

Evelyn looked up and merely smiled.

"Texans really love Texas," Kyle commented.

The waitress came to take their orders and drew Nicole's attention away from the back wall. Evelyn ordered the special and hot tea.

"I'll have a green salad with fresh lemon instead of dressing and an iced tea, please."

"With a straw," Evelyn added. "That's an awfully light lunch, Darlin'. It can't be more than twenty-five calories, if that. Why not get some Texas toast to go with it."

Almost afraid to ask, Nicole said, "What's Texas toast?"

The waitress chuckled. "It's just like ordinary toast, but much bigger. Texas style, ma'am."

"I see. Bigger, huh? I think I'll skip it. I'm still full from a late breakfast."

After the waitress took Kyle's order, Nicole asked, "You have to order straws?"

"Just with tea. If you had ordered a soft drink, you'd get one automatically," Kyle said.

Nicole shrugged in resignation.

They finished lunch, and Kyle paid the bill. As they were leaving the restaurant, the hostess called out to them, "Y'all come back, you hear."

Nicole turned around. "Thank you, we will."

She wondered why her aunt and Kyle sported such big grins when she took a quick step to catch up to them.

Evelyn took her arm. "You'll love the Gaylord Texan Resort. I'll tell you all about it while Kyle drives us there."

Evelyn talked nonstop as they drove down the freeway. "The Gaylord Texan is absolutely breathtaking. It's a resort and a convention center. The resort is situated high on a bluff overlooking Lake Grapevine. They have four acres of Texas vistas and landscapes. And a glass atrium. Best of all, they have Relâche. It's a European-style spa and salon and it's huge. I'm going to have Kyle drop me off at the resort so I can go to the spa while you two go on to the hospital."

Kyle broke into the conversation. "I'm partial to the safes in the rooms. They can hold laptop computers and have charging capabilities from inside the safe. They're really convenient."

The Grayson Children's Hospital and Research Center was also on the shore of Lake Grapevine, not too far from the resort. When they arrived after dropping Evelyn at the resort, there was a group interested in donating money to the hospital waiting for a guide. Kyle graciously volunteered to take them on a tour through the facility.

Nicole hung in the background, half-listening to Kyle's pitch, half-watching for bounty hunters to appear. He had a right to be proud of this facility. She had never seen anything like it. Each hospital room was a combination of living, dining, and sleeping. She liked Kyle's explanation.

"What does a child do when he or she is frightened in the night? He goes to his parent's room to sleep with them. Kids here are seriously ill and they're frightened. We encourage a parent to sleep over with the child. We've made the hospital rooms as homelike as possible with color and furniture. Parents are encouraged to stay with their child as much as possible. It makes a big difference in the child's speed of recovery."

The tour continued and at the end Kyle turned the group over to an assistant. "I have to go up to the critical care nursery for a while."

"Okay, let's go."

Kyle introduced Nicole to the pediatrician at the nurses' station adjacent to the nursery.

"Who's crying?" he asked the doctor, as he glanced through the window at the babies and looked at the bank of speakers.

"It's Mariah. She's five days out of heart surgery and not resting well at all."

"Call in a private duty nurse for her."

"Yes, sir. I'll take care of it."

"Nicole, I won't be long. Make yourself at home."

"We have plenty of time." Nicole smiled at him.

In an anteroom to the glassed-in nursery, Kyle scrubbed his hands and donned a sterile gown and mask before going to the crib and picking up the infant, who was swaddled in a pink blanket. "You're not alone, sweet girl," he soothed. "We'll just walk for a while." He put the baby up against his shoulder and rubbed her back gently.

"Does he come here often?" Nicole asked.

"Oh yes, several times a week when he's in town. He's a pretty special guy. We have standing orders to hire a private nurse and bill him if the family can't afford it. It's his belief children get better quicker if they're not alone, especially the infants. He says it's important they be touched and cuddled. And I agree with him." The doctor stood. "I have to go check on a few patients. There's a break room right next door, if you want something to eat or drink."

"Thank you, maybe later." She wanted to stay at the nurses' station so she could listen to Kyle as he talked to the baby. She sat back a little from the window and watched him walk Mariah. For the next half-hour he walked with her, singing to her softly and rubbing her back. Then he lowered the sleeping infant carefully back into her crib and watched her for a moment. As he turned to leave, she whimpered. He leaned over the crib watching her, but the whimpering didn't stop.

He took her back up in his arms. "All right, little angel. Maybe you're having a bad dream. I'll just rock you for a while." He sat down in the padded rocking chair and cradled Mariah in his arms, while he rocked the chair slowly and hummed a lullaby.

Nicole felt the sting of tears in her eyes and an ache in her throat. There's no way a man like this could be an embezzler. Someone really was framing him.

Ten minutes later, the private nurse arrived and exchanged places with Kyle.

"Sorry to be so long," Kyle said. "We have just enough time to get back to the resort and get spruced up," he said with a grin. "We may have to pry Evelyn out of the spa, though."

Nicole laughed at the comment. "No apology necessary."

In just a few minutes they were back at the resort and Kyle escorted her to the two-bedroom suite he had reserved for her and her aunt. He was in an adjoining single suite.

"I'll see you ladies in an hour or so."

"You go ahead, Dear," Evelyn said. "We might be a little longer. We'll meet you in the main ballroom."

"Okay, I'll watch for you," Kyle said and left.

It was close to two hours before Nicole and her aunt made their way to the main ballroom. Nicole was still stunned over the exquisite Christian Dior gown her aunt had given her. It was a pale-peach, jeweled gown which complemented Nicole's delicate coloring. As they entered, Nicole was glad to see security guards were checking invitations. The 30,000-square-foot ballroom was impressive. In addition to a stage large enough for a full orchestra, there was a broad dance floor, and hundreds of tables set with gleaming china and silver.

Kyle came to meet Nicole and Evelyn and escorted them to a table reserved at the front of the room, then excused himself to go to the stage and make a short speech.

"Welcome everyone. It looks like we have a full house and that couldn't make me happier. You'll also see pledge forms on your tables that I really hope you'll use. The Grayson Children's Hospital and Research Center desperately needs a new wing. To encourage you, I will match every pledge with an equal amount." Applause greeted his words. "I'm serious. This is your chance to break me. Do I have any takers?"

A man at one of the front tables stood and picked up the portable microphone on his table. "Well, Kyle, that's just too good an offer to pass up. I pledge five million dollars."

"Done," Kyle called. "I'll match it. Thank you, Mr. Winslow. Runners will pick up pledges at any time; just hold them up. Enjoy your dinner and the evening's entertainment."

The dinner was delicious. Nicole was glad she had taken Kyle's recommendation of the certified Angus beef steaks. Evelyn had chosen the Maine lobsters flown in the same day. They were casually sipping after-dinner coffee when Evelyn said she should mingle and encourage some more pledges.

The music started and Kyle stood and kissed Evelyn's cheek before offering his hand to Nicole. "May I have the honor of this first dance?"

"Of course." Nicole slipped her jeweled evening bag over her shoulder, smiled at him, and touched her aunt's arm as they passed her on the way to the dance floor.

Kyle took her in his arms and moved smoothly onto the dance floor. "You are incredibly beautiful in that gown."

"Why, thank you, and I think you've done a fabulous job here tonight."

"Not bad for a California boy."

"You're from California?"

He laughed at her surprise. "My dad was bringing in oil wells on our ranch while my mother was pregnant. She lost patience with the dirt and noise when she hit seven months, so Dad had her flown out to stay with her family in California." He shrugged. "But I was born early and Dad was brokenhearted. He changed the name of our ranch right after that so I'd always remember I was still a Texan. You've heard of being born with a silver spoon in one's mouth?"

"Yes, of course. Born wealthy."

"Well, our ranch was called Spurs, but Dad said I was born with silver spurs—no spoon in the mouth for a Texas cowboy. He renamed the ranch Silver Spurs so I'd always remember it."

"I think I'd like your dad. He sounds like a very strong-minded man."

"I'll take you—"

Nicole cut Kyle off as she caught a glimpse of a familiar face in the crowd. "Kyle! We're leaving. Stay behind me."

"What's wrong?"

She clung to his hand, dragging him through the crowd toward the doors. "I spotted Vishinsky in the crowd. He's one of the worst bounty hunters on the face of the planet. He's called Vicious and it's an apt nickname."

A tall, heavy, dark-haired man stepped in front of them. "Leaving so soon, Nicole?"

"Get out of my way, Vicious. This man is mine."

"Only if you can keep him."

Nicole swung her evening bag forward and flipped the clasp open just enough for Vishinsky to see the gleam of her Glock. "I don't think that'll be a problem for me."

Vishinsky's face darkened and he raised his voice. "You rotten bitch!"

Kyle moved before Nicole could stop him. He hit Vishinsky in the gut and followed with a left jab to the jaw, putting him on the floor. He signaled to security. "I think this man may be a troublemaker. Hold him somewhere for a few hours until he cools off."

The guards hauled Vishinsky away and Kyle apologized to the guests in the immediate area. "Sorry folks, an interloper with bad manners. I guess he doesn't realize he's in Texas."

A few chuckles greeted his remark and several men patted him on the back as he escorted Nicole into the hallway.

Nicole gave him a pained look. "We have to go to the nearest police department. I'm sorry. It's the only way I can keep you safe. Vicious never works alone."

Kyle nodded. He motioned to a security guard. "Have my car brought around to the garage entrance and tell Mrs. Parker her niece and I had to go to the Grapevine police department."

Kyle led her to the garage. "You drive," he said. "I know you're trained to handle these situations. I'll keep an eye out for trouble."

Nicole slid into the driver's seat while Kyle slipped in the passenger side. She started the car and pulled out of the parking garage. She followed Kyle's directions and was pulling into the parking lot at the Grapevine police department within ten minutes. As they walked toward the door, she touched his arm. "Wait."

He stopped and turned to face her. "What?"

She met his quizzical look with a serious one. "Before I turn you in, I want you to know I believe you're innocent. And if your lawyers can't find out who's setting you up, I will. I'll get you free as fast as I can."

His eyes softened. "Thank you." Then he grinned. "Does this mean I should fire them and hire you?"

She jabbed him in the side with her elbow. "Idiot," she muttered, but the word sounded more like an endearment. She knew he was joking to ease the tension.

He smiled as he took her arms, turned her to face him, and spoke softly in a delicious voice that sent shivers through her. "Thank you again, Nicole. I mean it." He nuzzled her face and lightly kissed her right cheek and then her left cheek before his chiseled lips closed over hers in a gentle kiss. She felt it all the way to her toes. It was a kiss that carried the promise of heat and passion to come—but not tonight.

He pulled back and gave her a rueful smile. "Let's get it over with."

They went through the door and the desk officer took one look at her gown and Kyle's tuxedo and referred them to the lieutenant on duty, who recognized Kyle. Seated at his desk, Nicole showed him her credentials and explained about the warrant. She gave the papers to the officer.

"Wait while I verify the warrant." The lieutenant entered information from the papers into his computer and initiated a search. "There's the warrant. Sorry, Mr. Grayson, but.... Wait a minute. It's gone! The whole thing just disappeared." He searched several files. "Everything related to this warrant is gone." He scratched his head, a perplexed look on his face. "I saw it momentarily so I know you're serious, but someone's playing games with you. Actually that's putting it mildly. Someone's hacked into the police network at the federal level. That's no game."

"Who could do that?" Nicole asked.

"Only a world-class hacker. It doesn't make sense. Grayson, an enemy of yours wouldn't create a warrant and then clear it. I'll make a report and let you know what I find out."

Nicole had a sinking feeling in her stomach as she contemplated the possibility of a friend staging this elaborate scenario.

They thanked the lieutenant and left. In the lobby Nicole sank into a chair. "Kyle, do you think Aunt Evelyn had her genius protégé set this up? I did come running when I got the warrant, and I wasn't going to get down here for the charity ball. Ev was really disappointed when I told her."

"Could be. I was thinking the same thing. Let's ask her." He gave Nicole his cell phone.

"Aunt Ev, it's Nicole. We're at the police department. The computer records on Kyle's warrant have suddenly disappeared." She motioned Kyle to share the phone so he could hear.

"Oh, that's wonderful news, Darlin'."

Nicole rolled her eyes. Kyle grinned and shrugged.

"Aunt Ev, could your protégé Jeffery have done this?"

"Certainly not! He's an honest boy. It's true he's very gifted. But he's only a student. And *I* am his teacher."

Nicole gasped.

"Are you still there, Nicole?"

"Oh, Aunt Ev..."

"Both of you come back to the resort," she said gently, ending the call.

"Oh my God," Nicole whispered. "My aunt is a world-class hacker." She pictured Evelyn being hauled off to jail. How many laws had she broken? Stricken, she looked at Kyle and almost wailed. "I don't know what to say."

"Well, I do."

Nicole's eyes widened. Kyle had every right to press charges. "What?"

"I say bless her heart. Bless her devious, conniving, matchmaker heart." He pulled Nicole to her feet and wrapped his arm around her shoulders. "I love her, too. And I'm glad you came running."

They walked toward the car and Nicole came to a halt and blurted out a horrified thought. "What if she gets arrested?"

Kyle laughed. "A world-class hacker? Not a chance. Anyway, I wouldn't let that happen."

In the car, she put her head on his shoulder. "Let's go. She'll be worried."

Kyle kissed the top of her head and wrapped one arm around her. "Yes, ma'am," he whispered.

Nicole, her face hidden in his shoulder, smiled.

Someday she would tell him she started to fall in love

with him when he couldn't bring himself to leave a baby
to whimper in her sleep alone.

But not tonight.

About the Author

Arline Todd resides in Euless, Texas where she is working on a romantic suspense novel and a futuristic series. Prior to this, the last position she held was as a director of marketing communications for a telecom company in Silicon Valley, CA. Arline has held a variety of positions, including operating room nurse, graphic designer, and advertising agency principal. She has an associate degree in engineering physics, a B.S. in technical journalism from Cal Poly, and an M.S. in mass communications from San Jose State University.